CRIES IN THE MIST

Book One of
The Briony Martin Mystery Series

STACEY COVERSTONE

Copyright 2012 by Stacey Coverstone
Cover Art by Sheri L. McGathy
Interior Design by www.formatting4U.com
Visit Stacey's Website at:
http://www.staceycoverstone.com

This is a work of fiction. Names, characters, places, and incidents are either the product of the author's imagination or are used fictitiously, and any resemblance to actual persons living or dead, business establishments, events, or locales, is entirely coincidental.

All rights reserved. No part of this book may be used or reproduced in any manner whatsoever without written permission of the author. This book is licensed for your personal enjoyment only. This book may not be re-sold or given away to other people.

Dedication

To my husband Paul,
who is always supportive and encouraging.

Acknowledgments

A big thank you goes to Melissa Blue and Mary Whealdon for taking their time to read this story and for their invaluable comments.

Chapter One

Briony's first glimpse of the lighthouse sent shivers racing down her spine. Shrouded mist clung to the sides of the tall structure that was as gray as the gloomy afternoon sky. She pulled her woolen cape closer to her body. Maine's freezing autumn held her in its iron grip.

Water pounded against the ferry's hull as it chugged toward Cape Marble. With her stomach churning, she stood at the bow gazing straight ahead at the waves crashing upon the approaching rocky shore of the small island. She sensed that nothing much had changed in these Atlantic waters from the beginning of time until this year of 1955.

Somewhere in the distance cutting through dark rolling clouds, seagulls cried. Adding to the already eerie atmosphere was the sigh of the wind that sounded like a woman moaning.

Briony reached into the bag hanging from her shoulder and dug out her father's binoculars. She raised them to her eyes and perused the lighthouse. It looked very old and weather beaten. Its paint was chipped. Cold and forlorn were more adjectives that came to mind as she moved the binoculars slowly up and down the building.

The structure stood on a narrow finger of land that jutted out from the island. It seemed the islet was barely large enough to support the tower with observation deck that rose from an immense oval base. Standing in its shadow set a small stone cottage. According to her father's letter, which was stowed safely in her purse, he was the keeper of the lighthouse. That, she found strange, since he'd been a medical doctor back in Kansas. Without warning, a blanket of fog obstructed her view, and she lowered the binoculars.

Stacey Coverstone

Reminding herself that she was on this journey solely because of his letter, Briony suddenly fought back tears. The long white envelope had been addressed to Ben Martin, her twin brother, who'd been dead for five years. According to her mother, the signature was definitely that of her estranged husband, who'd abandoned his family fifteen years ago, when Briony and Ben were only eight. Shocked and angered by the correspondence that was long overdue, her mom had hidden the letter when it arrived. If Briony hadn't been searching through the roll-top desk in the den for stamps, she might never have known about it.

She drew a deep breath of salty air into her lungs. It wasn't only the knowledge that her father was alive that had dragged her away from her quiet and familiar life in Kansas and brought her to this isolated destination. And it wasn't just to confront him with the pain his leaving had caused their family so long ago. Nor was it the mention of danger and a woman named Mira, who'd gone missing. What drew her to this unknown place was the urgency behind her father's words. The undertone of his missive was dark and mysterious, and he needed Ben's help.

"Formidable, isn't it?" A smooth baritone voice snapped Briony out of her musings. When she turned her head, the wind whipped her long hair into her face. She pushed the strands behind her ears and gazed at the man who stood at her elbow. Around six feet tall, muscled, and wearing a navy pea coat, he looked to be a few years older than her. Unlike the crew cuts and conservative styles of the day, this man's black hair was in a pompadour. His sideburns were thick and wide, and dark brows emphasized brown, sultry eyes.

"The island?" she asked.

"I meant the lighthouse. I've always thought it rather impressive and intimidating at the same time. In the colder months, it can be downright spooky." He extended his hand. "I'm John Fletcher."

Briony withdrew her hand from under her cape and

shook his, which was large and firm. "Briony Martin. Nice to meet you, Mr. Fletcher." She stuck her hand back inside where it was warm.

"Call me John." His brow lifted, and he gazed at her steadily. "There's not much of a reason for outsiders to find their way to Cape Marble unless they're attending a wedding, a funeral, or they're running from the law. Which category do you fall under?"

She wasn't used to such forwardness from a perfect stranger. Kansans were private people. But it would be rude not to converse. The two of them were the only people on the ferry besides a married couple with a little boy, and that family huddled together on a bench on the other side of the boat.

"I've come to visit my father."

"Where are you from?"

"Kansas."

"That's a long way to travel alone. You are alone, aren't you?"

She nodded.

"What's your old man's name?"

"Hugh Martin." Briony hadn't spoken her father's name in years. It sounded foreign on her tongue.

"I grew up on Cape Marble, but I don't believe I know him. How long has he lived on the island?"

Briony had no idea. The letter in her purse was the first correspondence he'd ever sent. For all she knew, he could have lived there for the past fifteen years. Or he could have traveled the world and recently found himself in the out-of-the-way spot that was only accessible by way of ferry or seaplane.

"To be honest, I haven't seen my father in many years. I don't know anything about his life on Cape Marble, except that he's the light keeper."

John rubbed his chin thoughtfully. "Really? They say ghosts haunt the island, including the lighthouse. Did you know that?"

Stacey Coverstone

"What?" Briony struggled to keep hysteria out of her voice. She freely admitted to having fears of everything outside of her safe existence, and believed all her fears stemmed from her father's abandonment and her brother's death. It'd been a hard enough decision to make this journey on her own—not to mention riding a train for the first time, and then a bumpy, crowded bus, and now this ferry; the only thing between her and deep, black, drowning waters. The last thing she needed to hear was that there were ghosts roaming around Cape Marble.

She was about to meet a father she could barely remember. Combine that building anxiety with the stress of the trip, and it was a strain to maintain her usual level-headed rationality. Anger that had been deeply buried was just now surfacing.

Briony hated her father for leaving them. She needed to look into his face and demand to know why he'd left his family in the middle of the night without so much as a note goodbye. She wanted to know why he hadn't he contacted them before now. Why had he given up his medical practice to become a light keeper? Had he thought of his family even once through the years? Did he regret leaving them behind to fend for themselves? There were so many unanswered questions.

He probably wouldn't be pleased to see that she'd come instead of Ben. But her brother was dead. Briony would have to do.

"Do you know him? The light keeper?" she asked her new companion.

He shook his head. "I've been away living on the mainland. I'm only returning home to take care of my old man's estate and clean out his house. He died recently."

"I'm sorry."

"Don't be. He was a hard-headed mule."

Briony bit back a smile.

"I hadn't seen or spoken to him in ten years," John said. "I guess you and I have something in common."

"I guess so."

The haze dissolved, and for a moment the sun broke through the clouds to give her a clear view of Cape Marble and the lone lighthouse. She raised the binoculars to her eyes again and positioned them on the dock ahead. No one waited at the landing. The captain had told her the boat only came twice a week and always at the same time. Disappointed, she'd thought her father might be waiting for its arrival each day, since his letter had requested her brother to hurry. Perhaps he was engaged with his lighthouse duties and would show up by the time they disembarked.

As she slowly moved the binoculars away from the dock and back to the tower, she noticed something she'd not seen earlier. She held the binoculars steady and squinted. It looked to be a small figure wearing blue standing on the observation deck. A woman! She clutched the rail. Her long dress blew out in a billow behind her.

Briony's father had mentioned a woman by the name of Mira. But he'd said she'd gone missing. So, who was this woman? Had Mira reappeared? It was possible, since it'd been nearly one month from the time Briony found the letter to now. Or was it one of those ghosts John had casually mentioned? Confused and taken aback, she lowered the binoculars from her eyes for a moment. When she raised them again and located the same spot, the observation deck was empty.

"Odd," she murmured.

"What's odd?" John's voice tore through her with a jolt.

"Nothing." Wishing he hadn't filled her mind with silly notions, she jammed the binoculars into the large bag hanging from her shoulder and nibbled her lower lip.

"What do you do in Kansas?" he asked.

"I'm a court stenographer." As soon as the words left her mouth, she regretted having given away so much of her personal information to a stranger. Mother had drilled into her that people couldn't be trusted, especially men.

Stacey Coverstone

John clasped his hands together and blew warm air into them. "I've seen my share of the inside of a courthouse."

When he said no more, Briony wondered at the comment. What did he mean by it? Was he a criminal?

"Prepare to go ashore!" the captain announced over a loud speaker.

The child who belonged to the married couple bolted to the rail and excitedly hopped up and down next to Briony. When he bumped her hand, her purse slipped from her fingers and splashed into the water.

"Oh, no! My purse fell overboard!" Tears of frustration blinded her eyes as she watched the leather bag sink in the depths of the dark churning water. The little boy looked up at her with wide eyes and then dashed back to his parents. John's sympathetic gaze met hers.

"Holy hell. What a stroke of bad luck that was. Will you be all right?"

"No, I don't think so. I've just lost my money, my address book, and my return travel tickets." *And my father's letter*, she thought, desperately trying to keep the hitch from her voice. She felt inside the pocket of her cape and felt a few folded bills and some coins her mother must have stashed there. It was small consolation, but at least she wasn't entirely broke.

John pointed to her square suitcase tied to the bench closest to them. "You still have your luggage. That's something, at least."

"And my shoulder bag," Briony relented. She squeezed the bag closer to her body and felt the hard shape of the binoculars against her rib. Maybe someone on the island would buy them from her. It was the only item of value with her that she could sell for money.

"Won't your father help you out with some cash?" John asked. "Surely, he'll buy your return tickets for you when it's time to leave."

She sighed. "Have you forgotten what I told you? I haven't seen him since I was eight years old. I don't know if he'll even be glad to see me." She excused herself and stepped toward the bench to retrieve her suitcase as a way of ending the conversation.

Chapter Two

When the ferry landed, Briony disembarked quickly and gazed around. Nobody waited on the dock. Her high heels clicked across the wooden planked bridge that led to shore. When she reached land, she released the breath she'd been holding. Finally she was off the water and on land again! As she set her suitcase on the ground, she wondered what her next move should be.

"Looks like your old man is a no show." John sidled next to her and then nodded to the married couple and their boy as they passed by and started up a short, steep hill.

"He doesn't know I'm coming. I'll go to the lighthouse and surprise him." Terrible at directions, Briony didn't know north from south or east from west. She lifted her suitcase and eyed the hill in front of her. When she took a step forward, John chuckled and reached for her arm to stop her.

"If you hike up that hill, you'll find yourself in the village. What little town there is, anyway. The lighthouse is that way. They're built close to the water for a reason." He pointed to his left and grinned.

She hated to be made a fool. She knew lighthouses were built near the water, but she was nervous and not thinking straight. Her lips pursed with mild annoyance. "Thank you." She marched past him and immediately felt her heels sink into the gravel path that led down to the sea.

John called out to her back. "Good luck with your old man!"

"I wish he'd stop with the old man business," she grumbled. When she craned her head over her shoulder a moment later, John was gone. Relief that his departure

Cries in the Mist

brought yielded to apprehension as she lifted her gaze and saw the top of the lighthouse jutting up through dark clouds. "I hope it's not going to rain." She quickened her pace and found herself in front of the stone cottage in short time.

She inhaled a deep breath and knocked on the door. Thinking she heard movement from inside, her heart started to pound with an insane rhythm. What would her father think when he saw her standing on his stoop? Would he even know who she was? When no one answered after a few moments, she rapped again. "Hello. Is anyone home?"

Her head pivoted at hearing the sound of a whistle, which she quickly determined was the wind. About a hundred yards from the house on the islet, and located down a short path made of broken seashells, stood the lighthouse. Briony stood motionless listening to the waves crashing upon rocks below it. Seagulls squawked and circled in the air above her. The sky rumbled with distant thunder. Never in her wildest imagination could she have pictured a more lonely and desolate place as this.

Her gaze slowly moved from the bottom of the gray tower to the top. Cool breeze touched her face in a gentle caress, like something alive. Suddenly an eerie sensation came over her, like someone was watching her. Briony's gaze flew to the observation deck. She thought about the woman in the blue dress she'd seen earlier. Had she imagined her before?

A cold snap of air drew her gaze away and caused her to hug her cape tighter to her body. She felt the pressure of the garters above her knees and suddenly had the desire to extricate herself from her stockings, heels, and the calf-length skirt she wore. It had been an exhausting trip. Soon it would be dark. Her stomach growled with hunger, and her body craved rest.

"Hello," she called again. She cupped her hands around her face and peered into the cottage window streaked with dirt.

The creak of the door stopped the breath in her throat.

Stacey Coverstone

It had opened about an inch. "Father?" She gently pushed the door open a little further. "Father, are you here? It's me, Briony." Again, there was no response.

Where was he? She'd never dream of entering someone's home uninvited, but this was the light keeper's house, wasn't it? And her father was the light keeper. Feeling she had no choice, she decided to go inside and wait. Anyway, she had nowhere else to go and night was falling. Surely her father would return soon.

She dragged her suitcase over the threshold, propped it against the wall, and shut the door behind her. The one-room dwelling felt cool and damp, and was as quiet as a tomb. Her gaze moved nervously to each of the four corners and flicked away from the shadowy walls. Fully expecting to see something staring at her with wild eyes, she cursed her imagination and sought out some light.

In the kitchen area, she found two kerosene lamps sitting on the counter next to the sink, as well as a box of long matches. After figuring out how to turn the wick up and down, she lit the lamps. The warm glow that radiated from them set her nerves more at ease and dispelled some of the gloom. She removed her cape and let her gaze drift.

The cottage was furnished simply. A cast iron kettle and frying pan sat on top of a wood-burning stove. A small refrigerator, a table covered with a red and white oilcloth, and two spindle chairs made up the kitchen half of the house. Upon quick inspection, Briony found some basic food staples in a cabinet above the kitchen sink.

On the other side of the room sat a brass bed in need of a good polish, as well as a lumpy sofa and a rocking chair. A few hardbound books lined a bookshelf on the wall. She peeked behind a door to find a toilet and narrow shower inside what she'd thought was a clothes closet.

Remnants of a female's touch was tucked in between the masculine furnishings: dried flowers in a vase on the table, a few oil paintings on the walls, curtains at the windows, and a pair of pink slippers on the rag rug next to

Cries in the Mist

the bed.

A small wooden dresser against the wall probably held her father's clothes, and perhaps Mira's, too. Whoever she was. Briony already felt guilty for nosing around, so she didn't investigate further. Although part of her wanted to confirm her suspicions that both male and female clothing filled the drawers, she didn't know if she'd be able to accept the truth—that her father had left them for another woman.

The reflection of glass on a bedside table caught her eye. With one of the lanterns in her hand, she walked to the bed and almost dropped the lamp. From inside a picture frame, her face stared back at her. In the photo, Ben stood next to her, with their father behind them with his hands clasped upon their narrow shoulders. She touched the frame, remembering that day. The photo had been taken at her and Ben's eighth birthday party. It was the last party their father had been at. He'd left a short two months later.

Briony's gut spasmed with the familiar pain of loss and anger. First, her father had gone without a word. Then ten years later, Ben had drowned in a river while vacationing with his best friend's family. Trembling, she turned her gaze from the photo and sunk onto the mattress, feeling drained.

It was then she noticed the wrinkled clothes lying on the bed. She picked up a shirt and held it to her cheek, trying to inhale some essence of her father. Why hadn't he told them goodbye? Hadn't he wanted to come see her and Ben at some time during the long years away? Couldn't he have written? Why had he sent for Ben now, after all these years? What was so urgent that his words had sounded so desperate? Some kind of danger threatened him. That much she was certain. If not, he never would have contacted Ben. But what was the danger? On the surface, Cape Marble seemed like a sleepy little seaside haven.

The screech of a restless wind and the rattling of the windowpanes caused her to jump. What had made her think she could come here on her own? Self-doubt rose like a viper and coiled around her heart. With the creepy sensation of being watched still plaguing her, the thought of confronting her father about his years of neglect didn't seem all that important after all. Suddenly she wanted to run and cocoon herself away in a safe place. But where would she go? It was dark outside now. She wouldn't know how to find her way to the village. Even if she did, she had no idea if there was a motel on the small island.

Briony felt so alone. The impression of someone close was so strong that she forced herself to look around. With her limbs trembling, she raised the lamp to her eyes and searched out the corners again. The scent of perfume clung strongly to the air. She hadn't noticed the sweet smell until now. Did the perfume belong to Mira? A cold chill washed over her, and the hair on the back of her neck prickled.

With the scent teasing her nostrils, she held the lamp tight so as not to drop it.

"Who's here?" she called. Of course, no one answered.

She perched gingerly on the edge of the bed and reached for calm, afraid to move. After what seemed like an eternity, the perfume scent dissipated, and her core temperature began to return to normal. Goosebumps still peppered her skin, but the icy feeling that someone had been in the room with her went away.

Briony stared at the photo again. Her father had asked for Ben, and he obviously knew the ferry schedule, so surely he'd turn up at the cottage sooner or later. She'd traveled all this way. It would be stupid and cowardly to leave now, before talking to him. Besides, her father needed her. And she needed to hear answers to her questions so that she could put the past behind her once and for all.

Feeling there were no options but to wait, she turned the wicks down on the lamps. Then she stretched out on the bed and laid her head on the pillow. Before long, her eyelids drifted shut.

Sometime later, what sounded like a rock hitting glass roused her. Rain drummed against the roof and slashed at the windows. They rattled wildly in their casings, caught in

Cries in the Mist

the fury of the burgeoning storm outside. She gazed around in the twilight to see that she was still alone. The flickering lamp on the bedside table gave just enough light for her to be able to check her watch and see that it was past midnight.

Where was her father? Why hadn't he returned home yet?

Another, louder crack against the window closest to the bed drew her full attention. She slipped off and tiptoed to the window and peeked out.

Standing in the rain, a man stared at her, a few yards from the cottage. She jerked her head back behind the curtain. Her heart began to thrash inside her chest. He wasn't her father. This was a much younger man with a crew cut. And he was getting drenched. Who was he, and what did he want? Not knowing what to do, she pressed her back against the wall and kept out of view. Another rock hit the glass. A moment later, a fist pounded on the door.

Briony jumped. Terror clawed at her stomach. Who would be calling on her father at this late hour? Was there a problem at the lighthouse? Or did this man have something to do with the danger her father had spoken of in his letter?

"Open up," the voice outside commanded. "I know you're there. I saw you in the window. There's no use trying to pretend no one's at home."

What should she do? Her mother's warnings and her own fears kept her rooted to her spot while she contemplated. The light from a jagged bolt of lightning sliced through the window to illumine the house, making her jump again.

"I need to talk to you," the man called. "It's about Wickie."

Wickie? Who was Wickie? Briony leaned against the wall, face sweaty, head hanging, and gasping for breath. She felt herself falling into the trance that often accompanied her bouts of panic.

"I know where your father is," the man said. "Let me in, and I'll tell you."

That wrenched her out of her stupor. She ran to the kitchen and slammed open drawers until she found a butcher's knife. With it held firmly in her grasp, she scrabbled for the door handle. When she yanked it open, the man's fist was raised in preparation to pound again. Water poured down his face and rolled off his yellow slicker onto his boots.

"Who are you?" she asked, wielding the knife in front of her.

His blue eyes enlarged. "Put down that knife and I'll tell you."

"No." Her heart beat faster, adrenaline sparking her wrists. "Tell me your name and why you're here in the middle of the night." She bounced on the balls of her feet, like a fighter.

His hands lifted in front of him, as if surrendering. "Okay, okay. My name is Alan Taylor. I'm just a fisherman. I came to tell you where Wickie is." His expression was as chilly as ice-kissed granite.

Her eyes narrowed. "Who's Wickie? I don't know anyone by that name."

The man wiped rain from his eyes. "I guess you know him as Hugh Martin. Around here, we call him Wickie. He's your father, isn't he?"

A knot twisted in her stomach. "How would you know that?"

"Can I step inside? I'm as wet as a drowned a rat."

Briony didn't like his analogy. Any mention of drowning resurrected sad memories of Ben. Although she knew better than to trust a stranger, holding the butcher's knife empowered her. She needed to know how this man knew Hugh was her father, and whether he really had information about his whereabouts.

"Turn your jacket pockets inside out," she demanded. He did so, and then she instructed him to slide his pants legs up and to turn around and show her his back pants pockets. When she was satisfied he had no weapons on him, she

Cries in the Mist

stepped aside and let him enter. He closed the storm out when the door shut behind him.

Briony took a couple of steps back and kept the knife trained on him. She perused his features and guessed him to be a couple of inches taller than her, around five foot six. Thinly built with golden hair, a scar cut across one eyebrow, and his face looked too weathered for his young age. "First of all, how do you know I'm Hugh Martin's daughter?"

"I ran into John Fletcher at the pub earlier this evening. He said he met you on the ferry and that you were the light keeper's daughter here for a visit."

John Fletcher. Briony's chest tightened at the thought of him. What gave him the right to share her business with anyone? Her temper flashed at him for being a gossip, and at herself for opening her mouth.

"It's a small island," Alan continued. "Everyone will know who you are by the light of day, anyway."

He was probably right about that. "Why do you refer to my father as Wickie?" she asked.

"That's the nickname given to early lighthouse keepers because they trimmed the wick on the lamp to keep it burning brightly. Someone apparently referred to your father that way when he first got here and it stuck. But I know what Wickie really was."

Briony blurted it out before she thought. "A doctor?" Alan's eyes crackled with rage, and a bad feeling bristled beneath her goose-fleshed skin.

His words spewed from his mouth like venom. "A murderer."

She swallowed the bile that rose in her throat and gripped the knife handle tighter. "That's a very serious claim to make, Mr. Taylor. What proof do you have?"

His hands clenched at his sides. "My dead sister, Sally. Is that good enough for you?"

"No, I'm afraid it isn't. I have no idea of what you're talking about. I'm sorry about the loss of your sister, but what does her death have to do with my father?"

Stacey Coverstone

Alan's teeth ground together. "He's the monster who butchered her."

Briony's head was already swimming. This accusation was like a punch to the stomach. Her voice came out small. "You're going to have to be specific, Mr. Taylor. What alleged role did my father play in your sister's death?"

The man's chest heaved in and out. "A lot of people know that he's the guy a girl goes to when she…when she gets into trouble. Sally couldn't raise a baby on her own, and the creep who knocked her up left the island. Wickie said it was a simple procedure. But Sally died on his table. When I saw her body, it looked like she'd been ripped apart by wolves." Angry tears glistened in his eyes.

Briony's fist flew to her mouth. This couldn't be true. When her initial shock ebbed, she said, "Are you telling me my father is an abortionist?"

"Was," Alan said, coldly.

"What do you mean was?"

The howl of the wind outside found the chinks and cracks in the walls of the cottage. Briony lowered the knife and wrapped her arms around her body, which began to shake uncontrollably. Foreboding rose like the tide when a great rumbling of thunder shook the house.

Alan's gaze seemed hewn in stone when he replied. "Wickie's dead."

Chapter Three

"I don't believe you." Briony choked back dizzying nausea. After all these years, it couldn't be. Her father couldn't be dead.

"It's true," Alan said. "As proof, I'll take you to his grave tomorrow when the storm's passed."

Grave? The reality of his words just about knocked her off her feet. If there was a tombstone with her father's name on it, there must be a body. It seemed clear. He father was dead. Distress flared inside her, burning up through her gut and exiting from her mouth in a strangled moan. In all her life, she'd never fainted before. But she felt she would now. Her legs wobbled beneath her, and the knife fell from her hand to clang on the floor.

Alan reached out and grabbed her around the waist as she felt herself slipping to the ground. He lifted her into his arms and strode to the bed. After laying her upon the mattress, he took it upon himself to fill a glass of water from the kitchen sink and handed it to her.

"Thank you." She sipped and eventually felt some life drain back into her body.

"I'm sorry to have blurted it out that way." Alan shook his head. "It's just that I've been so angry. Sally was my baby sister. She shouldn't have died. Wickie said it was safe. He said he'd done hundreds of them."

Still shocked at hearing that her father was dead and had been an abortionist, Briony scooted herself up against the brass headboard. "Are you certain she died from complications of the abortion?"

"What else could it have been? There was blood everywhere." His hands covered his face for a moment; his pain apparent.

"You saw her body and the blood?" Briony asked.

"Yes. Mira told me to wait outside, but it took too long. Finally, I lost my patience and burst through the door. I'll never forget the way poor Sally looked on that metal table with her body split open. I still suffer nightmares."

Briony glanced around the cottage and felt her limbs grow numb with cold. Had her father performed abortions here? She asked Alan.

"No. The surgeries were done in a room in the lighthouse."

A shudder rolled through her torso. Immediately, her thoughts returned to the woman in the blue dress she'd seen on the observation deck. "You said Mira told you to wait outside. Who is Mira?"

"Wickie's wife. She also assisted him with the surgeries. She's been missing for over a month. The Chief of Police believes there was foul play involved."

Mira was her father's wife? A bitter taste filled Briony's mouth. The union was common law if anything, and not legal, since he and her mother had never been officially divorced. "How do you know she's missing? Maybe she left the island on her own."

Alan shook his head emphatically. "One of her shoes was found at the base of the lighthouse stained with blood. Volunteers looked high and low for weeks, but there's been no sign of her whatsoever."

"How does the police chief know it was Mira's shoe?"

"It was hers all right. Three years ago, she contracted polio during that big nationwide epidemic. She was one of the more fortunate ones, however. She didn't die, but she did develop a mild paralysis that affected her legs. She wore special orthopedic shoes with braces to help her get around. Mira always wore long dresses to hide the shoes."

Long dresses? Briony inhaled deeply. "And how did my father die?" She prepared herself for the worst.

Alan leveled her with an intense stare. "The police

Cries in the Mist

chief ruled Wickie's death as a homicide. He was found behind this cottage with a bullet in his head."

Her heart nearly skittered to a stop. When her gaze fused with Alan's, she realized she'd dropped her knife when she'd felt faint. Vulnerability seeped into her bones. Maybe *he'd* killed her father. He certainly seemed angry enough to have committed murder. Perhaps he'd come here to kill her, too, out of revenge for simply being her father's daughter.

"Was anyone arrested for his murder?" she asked, trying desperately to control her emotions while subtly eyeing the knife on the floor.

"No." After a hesitation, he added, "I won't say I'm sorry he's dead. He claimed Sally hemorrhaged and it was a terrible tragedy that couldn't have been foreseen. But he murdered her as sure as if he'd strangled her with his own hands. Now he can't hurt any more girls. He got what he deserved, in my opinion."

Briony's ire rose. This man had said enough! She swung her legs off the bed and jogged to where the knife lay. She bent to retrieve it and held it at her side. "I think it's time for you to go, Mr. Taylor. Granted, I haven't seen my father in a long time, but I know the kind of man he is, or used to be. I don't appreciate your accusing him of murder, especially when nothing's been substantiated in the courts. A man is innocent until proven guilty. You should remember that before you go around sullying a person's reputation."

"He's dead. There's no reputation to uphold. And he can no longer defend himself to the courts."

"Exactly my point. Goodbye, Mr. Taylor."

When he hesitated to move, she raised the knife and nudged him toward the door with the sharp tip gently pressed against his arm.

"All right. I'm going." He flung the door open, and the rain seemed to have tapered off. Alan splashed into a puddle outside the door and turned around. "Do you want me to

Stacey Coverstone

show you Wickie's grave?"

If possible, she wanted nothing more to do with Alan Taylor. He'd scared her and accused her father of terrible things. Now he offered to show her the cemetery? No, thank you. He probably had plans to get her alone and hack her up. Her voice was stiff when she answered. "I'll locate it on my own."

He flipped the collar on his slicker up. "There's one cemetery on the island. Ask anyone in the village. They'll tell you how to find it."

She watched his back retreat into the mist and then closed the door with her heavy heart sinking to the bottom of her stomach.

~ * ~

Sunlight streamed through the windows the next morning, which suggested it would be a clear day. Briony had tossed and turned in the brass bed for the few hours she'd tried to sleep, haunted by nightmares of blood, death and ghosts. She needed a hot shower, a change of clothes, and some coffee to make her feel human again.

Since she now knew neither her father nor Mira would be returning to the cottage, she felt it was okay to make herself at home—at least until someone told her to leave.

After her morning ablutions, she heated a pot of coffee on the wood stove. She sat at the table and sipped the coffee while mulling over the few facts she knew. She also contemplated her reasons for staying on Cape Marble or going home immediately.

Her main objective—to meet and confront her father—was now moot. But how could she leave the island without knowing who'd murdered him and why? She couldn't. Although he'd kept secrets, hurt their family, and apparently lived a double life, he'd still been the father she'd worshipped as a child. She owed it to him to learn the truth about his death.

Cries in the Mist

Had he known someone bore a grudge against him when he wrote the letter to Ben asking for help? Perhaps he'd been threatened by Alan Taylor, or someone like Taylor, who'd blamed him for the loss of a loved one. Had Mira been abducted as a way of punishing Wickie? Why hadn't she turned up yet? Was she dead, too?

Briony wondered if her father had performed illegal abortions in Kansas. Could his leaving fifteen years ago been related in any way? Or had he simply suffered a midlife crisis, as her mother always suggested, and made a new beginning on this God forsaken island?

Realizing she'd get nowhere without learning more about her father's life in Cape Marble, she decided a visit to the police department would be the most logical place to start. She'd find out nothing unless she quietly conducted her own investigation.

Despite the sun casting its light across the landscape, the morning air was cool, so Briony wrapped herself in her cape. She plunged her hand into the pocket and rubbed the little bit of money between her fingers. Hopefully, she could make the cash stretch before having to sell the binoculars for the return fares home. She hated to think of parting with the only thing of her father's she had left.

As she closed the door behind her, an invisible thread seemed to pull her head to the right. Something unexplainable drew her toward the gray lighthouse. Broken seashells crunched below her feet as she trod down the short path. Once again, the isolation of the area robbed her of her self-possession. How her father had stood it here after the hustle and bustle of city life was difficult for her to understand.

When she reached the base of the tower, she remembered Alan Taylor's graphic description of his sister, Sally. The vision of a young woman lying bleeding on a table somewhere inside caused a tingle to move across her shoulders. Did she want to see the room in which her father had performed abortions? Not really, but a strange, almost supernatural stirring propelled her forward.

Her hand reached for the door handle to touch a padlock, which guaranteed no entrance. Relief flooded her body, as she hadn't wanted to go inside anyway. The lock had probably been installed by the police department as a way of keeping trespassers out after her father's death.

A thought occurred to Briony. Who was manning the lighthouse now? The woman she'd seen? A nervous laugh burst from her mouth when she realized there was no way she'd seen a woman in the lighthouse. The door was padlocked.

As she turned to walk away, the same flowery scent she'd smelled last night in the cottage enveloped her. With her hackles raised, she backed up a few steps. Her gaze lifted just as she heard a swish and a whoosh above her. A streak of blue disappeared around the corner of the observation deck.

Briony's gaze quickly shifted from the observation deck to the lantern room at the top of the tower. A faint, dark shape hovered beside the huge lens for several seconds. Then it was gone. She blinked, unsure of what she'd just seen.

"Good morning, miss."

Whirling, Briony's hand flew to her throat. A girl in a beige dress and white sweater stood on the path smiling. Amazingly, Briony hadn't heard anyone approach, which was weird, since her own footfalls along the seashell path had caused a terrible racket when she'd crunched over them. Perhaps she'd been too distracted by what she thought she'd seen in the lighthouse to notice someone drawing near.

"Sorry, miss. I didn't mean to frighten you," the girl said. She appeared to be sixteen or seventeen and had blonde hair that flipped up on the edges. Evenly cut bangs framed round pale eyes.

"It's all right," Briony answered, releasing a sigh. "I didn't hear you. You surprised me. That's all."

The girl glided past her with the elegant grace of a

Cries in the Mist

ballerina. Briony turned to watch her splay her fingers upon the base of the lighthouse. Then the girl withdrew her hand quickly, as if she'd been burned. Briony studied her discreetly, wondering if she was a neighbor. Although a gentle smile parted her lips, they held no color. She blended in perfectly among the dry weeds sticking up around the gray tower. Even the shade of her eyes seemed a bit washed out. She appeared as delicate and fragile as a baby bird.

"I didn't mean to disturb you," she said, sweetly. "You must have a lot to do. I won't bother you any longer. I just wanted to see who was living in the cottage now."

"Oh, I'm not living there," Briony said. "My father was the lighthouse keeper. Did you know him?"

The girl looked around her. Then her gaze lit on the door of the lighthouse and she blinked back tears. "He said everything would be all right. It wasn't. But it doesn't much matter now."

Briony heard a whistle seconds before she turned and saw John Fletcher striding down the path between the cottage and the lighthouse. She took a few steps toward him, wondering why he'd sought her out. He waved.

Annoyed with him for talking about her with Alan Taylor and God knew who else, she didn't wave back. She fully intended to give him a piece of her mind.

When she swung back around to excuse herself from the girl's company, her brow furrowed in confusion. The waif was gone.

Chapter Four

"Did you see her?" Briony asked John. Her head pivoted in a circle like a puppet on a string. The girl couldn't have just up and disappeared. There was no way past them except for the seashell path. There were sharp rocks below the lighthouse.

"Who?" he asked.

"A teenage girl. She was just here." Briony took a steadying breath, knowing she hadn't imagined her or their conversation.

When John shrugged, Briony decided to let it drop for the time being. She hadn't slept well, and her insides were raked raw. Perhaps she *had* dreamed her up. Anyway, scolding John took precedence over a strange girl.

He wore the same pea coat as yesterday and denims rolled up at the ankles. He smiled, and something behind his dark eyes hinted danger, but also passion. Briony ignored the way her stomach fluttered as she gave him the once over. Then she set her jaw, remembering she had a beef to pick.

"I don't appreciate your telling people about my business here on the island. I had an unpleasant midnight visit from someone called Alan Taylor. Are you going to deny you talked about me to him in a pub last night?" The tartness in her voice could have spiced a cherry pie.

John didn't skip a beat. He crossed his bulging arms over his chest, and his gaze looked straight through her. "No. I don't deny it."

"Well! At least you're an honest man." When she snorted, a laugh rumbled up from his belly.

"Alan was sitting on the bar stool next to me. I had a couple of beers and may have mentioned meeting you on the

Cries in the Mist

ferry. A beautiful woman can make a man lose his head and cause his mouth to have a mind of its own."

The next words caught in her throat. He thought she was beautiful? She felt her face heat. Suddenly, the anger leaked out of her as though someone had pulled the plug on a bathtub. Their gazes connected and fused. "Well," she said, softly. "I suppose I can forgive you this time. But don't let your tongue slip again or there'll be trouble."

John's mouth widened into a grin, and for the first time, she noticed the gap between his front teeth. Generally speaking, he wasn't what she'd call classically handsome, but he was attractive, nonetheless. She found him difficult to ignore. She'd never met such a confident man before. His devil-may-care attitude and rebel-with-a-cause appearance played havoc on her conservative mind-set.

Briony liked the predictable. John Fletcher was far from predictable. This magnetic pull she felt toward him was something to be fought, not embraced.

"Is there something I can do for you, or have you business here at the lighthouse?" she asked. Anxious to visit the Chief of Police and find the cemetery where her father was buried, her tone was short, but not rude. Being in John's presence set her nerves on edge.

"I came to see you." His face grew solemn. He pulled a notebook out from under his arm that she hadn't noticed until now. "Do you remember I told you I've come back to settle my old man's estate and clean out his house?"

"Yes."

"I found this in a locked trunk in the back of his closet last night."

Briony didn't understand what a notebook had to do with her. She waited for him to go on.

John tapped the notebook with his finger. "This is a record book. Inside are pages full of names. They're names of men who paid for abortions that your father performed. Some are local men. Most are from the mainland. The names have dates beside them and the amount of money paid. The names of the women receiving the abortions are also listed. Your father included notes about medical problems and that sort of thing. Did you know your father was an abortionist? You told me he was the light keeper."

Briony felt her heart turn over in her breast. She didn't understand what all this meant, but a dull awareness made the ache in her chest build. "There's nothing wrong with a doctor keeping a log of the procedures he performs." Even as the words left her mouth, she knew something more sinister was at play.

"Abortions are illegal, Briony." John scowled.

"Don't you think I know that?" she snapped.

"He was an abortionist covering as a light keeper."

The truth made her stomach roll with nausea. "I found that out last night. But how do you know?"

"Your midnight visitor, Alan Taylor, mentioned it at the pub. He also told me your father died."

"Murdered!" She narrowed her eyes. "Why was this logbook found under lock and key among your father's possessions?"

John shuffled from one foot to the other. "I don't know."

"Were he and my father friends?"

"I have no idea. As I said, I haven't spoken to my old man in years."

"They had to have been acquainted. Cape Marble is a small island. I would imagine everyone knows everyone. People in the village could confirm if they were buddies. I was on my way to the Police Chief's office. I'll ask him." Briony took a step forward, but John stopped her with a clamp on her wrist.

"I don't think that's a good idea."

"Why not?" When her gaze shot to his hand on her arm, he released her.

"Because the chief's name is one that's listed in this book. He's a married man. The woman's name next to his is not his wife's."

Cries in the Mist

She could see how that could open a nasty can of worms. "Then what should I do? I wanted to speak to him about my father's murder. Do you think he could have been involved? Maybe he found out about this record book and killed my father so the information wouldn't get out."

"That seems far-fetched, but not out of the realm of possibility. I know him. His name's Rick Pemberton. We attended school together when we were kids. I'm not sure how he got elected Chief. He always was a troublemaker. He's been in hot water before." John offered the notebook to Briony. "I think you should have this. After you've looked it over, I'd hide it in a safe place, if I were you. There might be others who don't want the information that they've paid for abortions to get out. One other name I recognized is Dennis Foley. He's the current mayor of Cape Marble."

Briony rolled her eyes. "Is he married, too?"

"I couldn't tell you."

She accepted the notebook with hesitancy. She was a logical woman, but also someone with fears of everything from spiders to things that went bump in the night. Her imagination ran wild when the notebook was placed in her palms. It felt hot to the touch. For a second, she wondered if the book had a curse upon it, but of course, that was ridiculous.

"I'm sorry about your father," John said.

"Thank you."

"What are your plans now?"

"I'm not sure."

He glanced at his watch. "I have a ton of things to do, but I hate to leave you alone with all this bad news."

"I'll be fine. I need to go to the village and find a market. Maybe the walk will help clear my head."

"I'm going. Do you want to walk with me?"

"Sure. Do you mind if we stop by the cottage so I can hide this notebook first?"

Once she'd stowed the logbook under the bed mattress, she and John made their way to the dock and hiked up the hill.

Cape Marble's main drag consisted of a half-mile of shops and businesses, including the police department and the town hall. Side streets dotted with trees covered in leaves of orange and red veered off of Main Street. The sidewalks were made of what appeared to be original cobblestones. Briony marveled at the adorable clapboard houses with gingerbread trim and white picket fences they strolled by, as well as the spooky Gothic Revival homes with pointed arches, steep gables and towers.

"Is your father's house here in the village?" she asked John.

"It's not actually a house. He lived above the pub. We own the dive."

"We?"

John clarified. "My old man owned the bar. That's where I grew up. Now that he's gone, it's mine. Not that I want it. I plan to sell the joint as soon as the estate is settled."

Again, Briony was reminded of the comment John had made on the ferry about his experiences with the legal system. Growing up on Cape Marble probably hadn't been easy. Living above a bar and being subjected to rowdy or drunken patrons didn't seem like the best childhood environment, in her opinion. And there probably hadn't been much to do as far as recreation on an isolated patch of land in the middle of nowhere. Perhaps he'd gotten in trouble and his father had shipped him off to the mainland to a military school, or an institution for juvenile delinquents. Perhaps that was the reason they'd been estranged.

The low, rich sound of his voice interrupted her musings. "The pub is three storefronts down that way." He pointed in that direction. "I've got a lot more cleaning to do and stuff to go through." In an intimate gesture, he leaned toward her and traced the curve of her jaw with his finger. The touch of his warm finger against her chilled skin sent heat crawling up her neck. "Be smart if you're determined to snoop around and ask questions. Mainers are suspicious people by nature. They don't like outsiders sticking their nose into their business. It could spell trouble if someone thinks you're out to cause them harm."

"If you're trying to scare me, you're doing a good job," Briony said. His liquid eyes held mystery and a little danger, but it wasn't a far stretch to imagine them filled with longing, as well. A longing she wouldn't encourage.

"All I'm saying is to be careful. Someone murdered your old man and may have killed his wife, or girlfriend, or whoever she was. If you need someone to talk to an help sort through things later, look me up." He winked and turned on his heel.

"John!"

"Yeah?" He craned his head over his shoulder.

"I hate to ask you this, but I hope you'll understand why I must. Is your father's name in the record book?"

His jaw twitched. "No." With that simple statement, he threw her a backhanded wave and sauntered down the sidewalk.

Briony exhaled a gentle rush of air. She'd see for herself when she examined the book, but she'd wanted to gauge his reaction when asked the question. Her heart picked up its pace. She didn't know if the erratic beats were due to his dire warnings or the way she'd sizzled inside when he stroked her face and gazed into her eyes. She hadn't much experience with men in a romantic way. In spite of her misgivings and her mother's lifelong warnings about men, John intrigued her.

She snapped her fingers. She'd meant to ask him where the cemetery was located. Gazing down the walk, she realized he'd already vanished. Another thought came to her suddenly. He'd mentioned Mira, but she hadn't. If he'd been away for a long time and had just returned to the island recently, how did he know about her? Maybe Alan Taylor or someone else at the pub had mentioned Mira being missing. Apparently, Mr. Taylor had a big mouth. Or perhaps John knew more than he wanted to acknowledge. Although she thought she'd felt a spark ignite between them, something hinted she'd be wise not to trust too soon.

A bell tinkling from next door grabbed her attention. A laughing couple exited the door of a diner. Wonderful smells wafted outside to tickle her nose. Having had nothing to eat since yesterday except coffee this morning, Briony was starved. Perhaps she could kill two birds with one stone: have breakfast and fish for information about who might have held a grudge against her father.

The diner was crowded. She was well aware of the stares she received as she sat at the counter on a metal stool covered in red leather. A redheaded woman in a form-fitting pink uniform took her order. From the prices on the menu board, Briony determined she could afford an egg and toast. "And a glass of water, please," she added, hoping it wouldn't cost extra.

"Coming right up." The waitress stuck her pencil behind her ear and put the order in. Then she set the glass of water in front of Briony. "You're not from around here, are ya?"

"No." She smiled politely. "I'm just visiting."

"I've lived here all my life. Who ya visiting?"

Briony cleared her throat. She hadn't expected to talk about her father so soon. "My father."

"Oh? What's his name?"

"Hugh Martin. People around here called him Wickie, I'm told. He is—was—the lighthouse keeper."

The waitress, whose name was Liz from the tag pinned on her dress, froze. Her perky smile dissolved. Briony swore she saw the color drain from her face.

"Did you know him?" she asked.

Liz's mouth twitched. "Sure. We all knew Wickie. I'm sorry for your loss."

"Thank you. Did my father eat here in the diner?"

"Oh, yeah, off and on. I don't think his wife, Mira, was much of a cook. Things most of us take for granted became

Cries in the Mist

even harder for her after she contracted polio. And the keeper's cottage doesn't have modern conveniences."

Briony winced at hearing Mira called his wife. Although her mother had moved on with her life years ago, Briony still dreaded having to be the one to tell her the news of her father's other relationship and secret life.

"I'm visiting from Kansas," she said, continuing the conversation in hopes of reeling in some information. "My father was a physician there many years ago."

Liz ran a wet rag over the counter top. "I didn't know that."

"He never mentioned his former occupation?"

She chewed her lip. "People around here like their privacy. Most of us raised on Cape Marble want to get off this rock, so when someone moves here, we don't ask questions. Think about it. Why would anyone want to settle on this desolate island, unless they're hiding from something, or someone?"

The truth of Liz's remark felt like an arrow to Briony's heart. "Do you remember when my father arrived on Cape Marble?"

Liz's coiffured eyebrow arched. "Don't you know?"

"Unfortunately, he and I have been estranged."

"Oh. Well, let's see. I think he arrived on the island twelve, thirteen, fourteen years ago. Something like that. I was in elementary school at the time, but it's easy to remember newcomers because they're few and far between."

The timing was right. When he left Kansas, his plan must have been to come directly here. But why? What, or who, drew him to this part of the world? She couldn't imagine. "Liz—may I call you Liz?"

"Sure."

Briony leaned forward and lowered her voice. "Liz, I'm sure you overhear a lot of talk here in the diner. Do you know if my father had any enemies? Was there anyone on the island who might have wanted to hurt him?"

Stacey Coverstone

The waitress forced a smile that didn't seem genuine. "I don't eavesdrop. Anyway, the police talked to practically everyone already. Apparently, they have no suspects and no motive. Why would a simple light keeper have any enemies?"

Was it possible she really didn't know about Wickie's other occupation? Or maybe she honestly didn't know who would want to kill a simple light keeper, as she put it. "That's what I'd like to find out," Briony answered.

"Order up!" The grill cook glowered at Liz through the server's window.

She set Briony's plate in front of her and then excused herself. "I can't talk anymore or I'll get fired. And I can't afford to lose this job."

Briony felt she was hiding something. "I understand. Thanks for talking with me. If you think of anything that might help me in learning what happened to my father or Mira, would you contact me? I'm staying at the cottage."

Liz looked around nervously and then whispered, "I'd suggest you take the next ferry out and go back to where you came from. There are secrets on this island that people want to keep buried. If you dig too deep, you might end up in a grave next to your father, the *lighthouse keeper*." She accentuated those last two words.

Briony nearly choked. Suddenly, she lost her appetite.

Chapter Five

Briony paid for her half-eaten meal, then the cashier gave her directions to the cemetery, located on a bluff overlooking the ocean. It was a pretty spot, despite exposure to the elements. She pulled her cape tight to ward off the cold wind that whipped about her hair and chilled her bones.

The grave was fresh and therefore easy to locate. With autumn fully in swing, there would be no grass upon the burial site until next spring. The mound looked barren. Briony wished she'd stopped at the florist's shop and purchased a small bouquet of flowers, even if it had meant sacrificing what little money she had.

She stood at her father's tombstone and let the tears fall. First she had a father, then she didn't, then she did again. Now, he was gone forever. It seemed some monstrous force had been toying with her all her life. As her finger traced the engraved letters of his name, her pent-up anger disintegrated. But the sadness remained.

He'd been a great dad to her and Ben when they were children. He'd never abused their mother, as far as she knew. Mom had adored him in those days. Whatever had gone wrong and drove him away was something Briony would never understand and had no hope of ever discovering. Apparently, it was a secret he'd taken with him to the grave.

There was no point in holding onto past hurt. It was too much to ask her to completely forget the pain she'd suffered by his abandonment, but she could forgive him. From this point on, she'd try to remember only the good times they'd shared together. The really terrible thing was that a monster had snuffed out her father's life just when she'd been so close to reconnecting with him. That she wouldn't forget, and couldn't forgive.

"Father, I promise to find out who did this to you. Even if it takes me the rest of my life, I swear I'll track down your killer and see that justice is served."

As she briskly trekked back to the village, her thoughts were as scattered as the brittle autumn leaves flying around. When she passed the pub, she glanced into the big front window wondering if she'd see John inside. Then she remembered that his father's apartment was above the tavern. There was no quelling her urge. She looked up hoping he might move in front of the window at that exact moment and she'd catch a glimpse of him. When she bumped into what felt like a brick wall, she let out a small shriek.

A man wearing a blue uniform, a brimmed cap, and a silver badge on his jacket lapel glowered at her.

"Excuse me!" she exclaimed, pressing her hand to her heart. "I didn't see you there."

"That's obvious."

Briony read the inscription on his badge: Police Chief. What a coincidence. She stared into his eyes and shivered. He looked unfriendly. And he'd paid for an abortion for someone other than his wife. Had he also murdered her father to keep that knowledge from leaking into this small community?

She'd wanted to ask him questions about the investigation into her father's death, but John had convinced her it wasn't a good idea. It was a suggestion she now agreed with. The chief's pocked face seemed fossilized into an expression that would intimidate someone far less frightened by life than her.

"You're Wickie's daughter, am I right?" His voice sounded like gravel.

"Yes. Yes, I am." There was no use in denying her identity. Alan Taylor had told her that everyone on the island would know her by the morning light.

Cries in the Mist

"Rick Pemberton, Chief of Police." He extended his hand. "Sorry for your loss, miss."

She shook and felt he could have cracked all the bones in her hand with one big squeeze, if he'd wanted to. "Thank you, Chief." She hadn't expected condolences, so she bucked up her courage and decided to broach the subject after all. "Have you any suspects with relation to my father's murder?"

A frown appeared between Pemberton's bushy brows. "About that. I'm afraid the coroner made a mistake."

"What do you mean?"

"The corner initially suspected homicide. Now he's declared Wickie's death was a suicide."

"Suicide?" Briony couldn't believe her ears. Pemberton's eyes narrowed, as if daring her to contradict him. "How could such a mistake have been made?" she asked.

He rubbed a hand over his chin. "Believe me, Miss Martin, I've asked that very question a dozen times now. Shoddy work is all I can come up with. You'll be pleased to know the man has been released from his position. He's already left the island."

Briony wasn't sure if she was pleased by this information or not. Something didn't ring true. How could an official coroner's report change a couple of weeks after the body had been buried? She didn't believe her father had committed suicide, but she wouldn't let the chief know her doubts. He glared at her with eyes as cold and hard as bullets.

"I'm sorry for the bad news," he said. "You've been to see his grave already."

It wasn't a question. How did he know? Did he have people following her? Twice she'd sensed someone watching. It felt like eyes bore into her right then. "Yes, I just returned from the cemetery."

"Good. Then you've said your goodbye. There's no reason for you to stay on Cape Marble any longer. The ferry returns in two days. You'll want to be on it when it departs."

Was that a threat? Anger flared in her stomach. Obviously, there was something Pemberton didn't want her to discover. If it was the abortion he'd paid for, she already knew about that. But he didn't know she knew. He must have felt he could bully her into leaving. She'd thought she could be coerced easily, too, until this moment.

Shoulders stiff with rage, blood surged through her like a speeding train. She'd come here because her father had sent the letter seeking help from home. Before he'd gotten that help, someone had murdered him. Hadn't she just promised him justice?

She reached for calm and kept her words measured when she responded. "Thank you for the ferry schedule, Chief Pemberton. Even though I arrived to unpleasant news, I've found Cape Marble to be a charming little place. I believe I'll stay on a while longer. I must run now. It was a pleasure to meet you."

She nodded and strode past him with a smile quirking the corner of her mouth. Pride bloomed in her chest. It felt good to hold her own against such an intimidating presence. *One baby step at a time*, she told herself.

Briony stopped by the market and picked up a couple of apples as well as bread and cheese for making a grilled cheese sandwich on the wood stove. She had no idea how long she'd actually be staying on the island, and hoped if she were frugal, her meager money would last. There were a few things in the cottage to eat, but she felt strange partaking of them with her father dead and Mira missing.

When she exited the store, she noticed a woman standing across the road staring at her. Petite with a scarf tied around her head to keep her hair from getting mussed, the trench coat she wore was belted tight around a tiny waist. Her face looked pale from this distance. Briony offered a quick smile and then started down the cobblestone walk toward the hill that led to the dock.

"Miss Martin!"

Cries in the Mist

Briony stopped and turned. The woman's high heels clacked along the cobblestones in discreet pursuit. Who was she, how did she know her, and what did she want?

"You *are* Miss Martin, aren't you?" The woman sidled next to her, and Briony whiffed the popular scent of Chanel No. 5 emanating from her skin. Up close, she looked older than what her actual age probably was. The scarf slipped back from her forehead to expose hints of gray in her hair. And the thick layer of powder on her face couldn't hide the crow's feet that extended from the corners of her melancholy eyes, or the dark circles beneath them.

"Yes," she answered. "I'm Miss Martin. How can I help you?"

The woman's gaze darted around them. Her voice dropped to a whisper. "Could we speak in private?"

Noticing a small white church at the end of the street, Briony suggested they talk there, where they could get out of the cool air.

Once the door was closed behind them and they saw there were no other people in the sanctuary, the woman led Briony to the closest pew and they sat. She sighed deeply.

"I just saw you speaking to my husband, Miss Martin. Don't think I was spying," she added quickly. "I happened to be coming out of the five and dime when I saw the two of you on the sidewalk."

Briony's hand shot out from under her cape to shake. "It's a pleasure to meet you, Mrs. Pemberton."

"Please call me Violet."

"All right, Violet. What can I do for you? And how did you know my name?"

The wisp of a smile crinkled the corners of her thin lips. "It doesn't take long for folks around here to learn a stranger's name, Miss Martin. We don't get many visitors to Cape Marble, especially this time of year. When we do, it's big news."

"So I've been told. By the way, feel free to call me Briony."

"Oh. What an unusual and beautiful name."

"Thank you. Now, how can I help you?"

Violet's mouth turned down. She began to wring her hands in her lap. "I wanted to ask you, woman to woman, not to lead my husband on. I'm fully aware of his many indiscretions through the years, and I'm tired of being made a fool. This time I've decided to face the problem head on. I can't take any more humiliation."

Taken aback, Briony saw the depth of pain that entered her eyes. But she wanted to set things straight immediately. "Mrs. Pemberton—Violet—I assure you, there's nothing for you and I to discuss in this regard. I have *no* interest in your husband whatsoever, except in a professional sense. I only just met the man, and we were talking about the investigation into my father's death. Surely you heard that he died recently. He was the lighthouse keeper."

"Yes, I heard. So, Rick didn't proposition you?"

"Of course not!"

She exhaled, but didn't look completely convinced. "That's a relief." Her gaze latched onto Briony's again. "That doesn't mean he won't try."

"I promise, Violet, your husband could be Casanova himself, and I wouldn't allow myself to fall for his charms. I don't date married men." *Particularly bullies*, she thought. *And ugly ones with secrets, at that.*

Violet changed the subject abruptly. "Don't let my husband fool you into believing Wickie wasn't murdered, because he was."

Goosebumps peppered Briony's skin. "How do you know?"

"I know."

"But how?"

Before Violet could say more, a loud crash from the front of the church made them both jump. Violet screamed, "Ghosts!" Then she leaped up from the pew and bolted out the door, slamming it behind her. Briony followed suit, but when she stepped outside and looked in all directions, there

Cries in the Mist

was no sign of the chief's wife.

~ * ~

Back at the cottage, while eating her grilled cheese, Briony stared out the window at the sky that threatened more rain. The logbook that had belonged to her father was sitting on the sofa next to her, but she hadn't yet read what was inside. Every time she touched the cover, it seemed she could hear the cries of unborn babies echoing in her ears. So, she ignored the notebook and thought about what Violet had said instead.

Was the chief's wife to be trusted as a reliable source of information? She'd seemed sure that Wickie was murdered. But she'd also acted nervous and paranoid. Briony suspected Violet might be a few cards short of a deck—as the saying goes.

According to Mrs. Pemberton, her husband was a serial adulterer. But did that make him a murderer? Briony was interested in knowing if Violet knew of the abortion he'd paid for. Maybe the mousy woman had been putting on an act today. What if she'd discovered her husband's transgression and confronted Wickie or Mira? An abortion for the woman he'd gotten pregnant would wipe away any evidence of infidelity. In a twisted way, she might have blamed them for allowing him to get away with cheating on her.

Could Violet have killed Briony's father? Was it possible that a wolf hid under that frail little sheep's clothing? In the mystery books she'd read, it was usually the quiet and least suspecting person that ended up committing the crime. It was a theory worth more consideration.

Finally, she screwed up the courage to open the logbook and read down the list of names and dates. She stared open-mouthed in shock at the number of pages that were filled with men who had paid for abortions in the past fifteen years and the women who had undergone the procedures.

Her stomach lurched when Rick Pemberton's name popped out. Recorded on his line was the patient's identify, Jennifer Lee, whoever she was. Further down was Alan Taylor's name shown as having paid for his sister, Sally's, surgery. Briony's interest was piqued when she came across the name of Dennis Foley, with the words *Cape Marble Mayor* scribbled next to it. She remembered John mentioning the mayor's name. Disappointingly, the identity of the woman whose abortion he'd paid for was smudged and illegible. However, the procedure had taken place only two months ago. In her opinion, that made him a possible suspect, because of the timing of her father's death. A man in such a position of authority wouldn't want it known that he'd gotten a woman pregnant and paid for her to have an abortion.

Nearly all of the other names were of men and women who had traveled from the mainland to procure Wickie's services, confirmed by their off-island addresses written in the comments column.

Briony closed the logbook and sniffled. It seemed apparent that her father had left Kansas to come to this faraway spot in order to perform abortions without the fear of being found out and arrested. According to the fees he'd charged, he must have died a rich man. She hoped leaving his family had been worth it all.

Her gaze flew to the slippers on the floor next to the bed. She wondered how long it had been before he'd taken up with another woman. Frustrated by the complexities of the man she thought she'd known and her own conflicted feelings, she pounded her fist upon the sofa. Mira may have shared his home and his bed, but in the end, it had been his son he'd asked for. That was Briony's only consolation that her father had not been as heartless as it appeared.

With emotion clogging her throat, she bounded up from the sofa and stretched her legs. Then she stepped outside for some fresh air. The scent of approaching rain

Cries in the Mist

dampened her skin, and the distant rumble of thunder signaled another storm was on its way. From this vantage point, she could hear the rolling sea and the waves crashing upon the rocks below the lighthouse. Gulls squawked and wheeled around in the sky.

She could also see the top of the lighthouse clearly. Confused, she watched dumbstruck as the lamp flashed on and off and on again. This morning, the tower door had been locked.

An icy feeling slid up her arms. She gulped. Through a veil of mist, she saw a woman's figure silhouetted against the blinding beacon of light.

Chapter Six

Before stopping to think, Briony ran down the seashell path to the lighthouse. She rattled the padlock on the door.

"The light isn't automated. Who turned it on? And how did they get inside?"

With her heart galloping, she backed away from the base of the tower and gazed upward. A woman's face stared at her from the lantern room. From somewhere inside, a door slammed.

The same fragrance she'd smelled in the cottage last night materialized from out of nowhere and swirled around her head. Briony stumbled to the door again and shook the lock with all her strength. She had to break the lock and find out who was inside the lighthouse! Maybe it was Mira.

She ran around to the other side of the tower and searched for a big rock in which to bust the padlock with. In her haste, her feet slipped out from underneath her. As a scream burst from her mouth, she slid on the grass and down the sloping bluff. Digging the heels of her shoes into the ground, her hands snatched at the loose earth. When her body jolted to a stop, she gasped for breath. Sea spray misted her face. Waves pounded the rocks below.

Briony slowly scooted backwards on her elbows and rear end until she was in no further danger of falling over. Her chest heaved. If she'd gone over, she would have died, and no one would have known. The pulses in her neck and wrist throbbed like drum beats, but there was no time to think about what ifs. She scrambled around until she located a heavy rock and then ran to the tower door.

It took a dozen hard whacks, but she finally broke the padlock. The hinges creaked when she pushed the door

Cries in the Mist

open. For a woman who preferred a calm and quiet existence, she swallowed past the tightness in her throat and armored herself against the fears that had ruled her most of her life. Mentally, she prepared herself to confront the unknown.

Once inside the entry, she stepped to the bottom of the spiraling staircase and looked up into the darkness toward the lantern room. The perfume filled her senses again, compelling her to follow it. As she mounted the stairs, the fragrance completely enveloped her. The higher she ascended, the more intoxicating the scent became.

The tread of her footsteps on the stairs echoed through the tower. Or were they someone else's footfalls she heard above her? Panic quivered in every cell of Briony's body, but she refused to retreat. Learning the identity of the woman she'd seen looking at her from the lantern room was more important than the feeling that her heart was about to explode inside her chest. If the woman was Mira and she'd been hiding in the lighthouse all this time, Briony intended on finding out why.

The moment she reached the lantern room, the lamp went off. She grasped the handrail when something whooshed past her. Her body went numb. It felt like a bucket of ice water had been thrown at her. A woman's shriek gave wings to Briony's feet.

To hell with bravery!

She raced back down the spiral staircase feeling like there were hundreds of eyes upon her. When she reached the bottom, her gaze was drawn to her left. Her breath was shallow, and her heart skipped beats. As if an invisible hand were pushing her, she walked around the corner and down a short hallway. It was no surprise to discover a closed door at the end of that short hall. Somehow, she knew what she'd find inside.

Before she lost all nerve, she flung open the door and stepped into the room that lay in shadows. It took a moment for her eyes to adjust to the dim. When it did, her gaze moved around what had obviously been her father's surgery chamber.

More like a chamber of horrors, she thought, with a shudder. There were no windows in the room, and the walls were painted the same dingy gray as the outside of the tower. Her gaze landed on the metal table in the middle of the room. There were stirrups attached to the end of it and metal restraints clamped to the sides where the patient's wrists would be. A large spotlight wired to a tall pole at the foot of the table apparently provided enough light for the surgeries.

She forced her feet to move closer. As she examined the tray of medical instruments on a roll cart, her hand flew to her mouth. Some of the tools were stained with blood. Bloodstains were also evident on the concrete floor.

Plastic gloves, surgical masks, and paper sheets were found in boxes on another metal cart nearby. Briony turned back to the operating table and touched it. The metal was as cold as ice. She noticed a space heater against one wall, but it couldn't have heated the area well, especially in the bitter wintry months.

Imagining hundreds of women lying on the table in this unsterile environment, half naked, while her father killed and disposed of their babies made Briony sick. Bile crawled up her throat. She bent and braced her hands on her knees, feeling like she would wretch. Perspiration dampened her brow. Her stomach convulsed, but she only dry heaved.

When the nausea finally passed, she gulped in air, which was not fresh, and decided she'd seen enough. As she stumbled toward the door, the distant echo of crying babies stopped her in her tracks. In a slow crescendo that sounded like rumbling thunder, the sounds grew closer and louder until the wailing filled the room.

She covered her ears to drown out the haunting cries. The walls around her felt like they were closing in. The presence of the spirits of unborn children was frightening and so strong. The smell of soured milk invaded her nostrils.

Cries in the Mist

She could practically feel the babies' sharp little fingernails scratching at her skin.

The atmosphere in the room thickened. The crying grew to a frenzied pitch. She felt she might suffocate if she didn't get out of the room. Using her hands as shields, she pushed through what felt like a solid wall of bodies and flew down the hall and out the front door. In her haste to get away, she forgot to shut the door behind her.

She raced up the seashell path with the terrifying sensation that the babies were chasing her. Although her logical mind told her none of it could have been real—the perfume, the woman's face, the crying babies; that it had all been a trick of the mind caused by stress and exhaustion— there was no way she'd look over her shoulder. She might die of fright if she did.

When she reached the cottage, her feet skidded to a stop. Her eyes widened. The young girl from this morning waited on the stoop. She wore the same beige dress and white sweater. Her strange disappearing act earlier flashed through Briony's mind. The girl had rotten timing. Briony was in no mood for a visitor.

She forced her body around, and she glanced down the seashell path. After inhaling deeply several times, Briony caught her breath. The only thing that had followed her up from the lighthouse was a squirrel carrying a nut in its mouth.

Reeling from the terror that clawed at her insides, she swallowed her fear and forced politeness from her voice. "Hello again."

"Hello." The girl smiled and then stared into the cottage window.

Briony moved closer. "Can I help you with something?"

"No. I've been here before."

"I know. It was just this morning."

"Before that," the girl said.

"Is that so?" Briony wondered if the girl had consulted

with her father regarding an abortion. If so, she was far too young for that sort of thing.

"Why did you leave so quickly this morning?" Briony asked.

The girl's pale eyes seemed to look straight through her. "I could only stay a moment. Those are the rules."

"The rules? Whose? Your parents?"

The girl's hair bounced on her shoulders when she shook her head. Then her eyes rolled upward toward the sky. "His."

Briony looked up. Dark clouds rolled by. "His? Do you mean God?"

The girl giggled and nodded.

Briony sighed. It was obvious the young woman was either very immature or she suffered from a mental deficiency. Perhaps everyone suffered from some sort of mental problem on this rock. The weather and isolation was enough to drive a person crazy, as she was becoming well aware. "Would you like to come inside for some tea?" she asked, feeling tea would soothe her own raw nerves.

"No. I should go now. Goodbye."

"Wait. Before you leave, would you tell me your name? Mine's Briony Martin. Maybe we could be friends."

"Okay. I'm Sally Taylor."

Every nerve in Briony's body hummed. "S..S...Sally...Tay..Taylor?"

"Bye-bye," the girl said, cheerfully. She turned and strolled down the path toward the lighthouse. The hairs on Briony's arms stiffened when she saw that the back of her dress was covered in blood.

When the girl stepped through the solid concrete base of the lighthouse and vanished in front of her eyes, Briony flung open the cottage door and bolted it behind her.

~ * ~

Thirty minutes later, she knew she couldn't sit in the

Cries in the Mist

cottage any longer, or she'd go nuts trying to reason out the unreasonable. All logic defied the supernatural things she'd been experiencing. Briony had to talk to someone about what was happening!

John had mentioned ghosts on the ferry. He would be the most logical person to confide in. But Sally Taylor had shown herself twice now. Why? Maybe it was a sign. Perhaps she wanted Briony to reach out to her brother, Alan. Briony decided to find him. She remembered him telling her he was a fisherman, so she slipped on her cape and headed for the dock.

An old man she spoke to pointed out boats bobbing in the water and a scale house a hundred yards down shore. "You might find Alan there weighing his catch."

Briony did find him there. She waited off to the side until Alan had transacted business and received some cash from a man in rubber boots and a sailor's cap. Then she approached him.

"Excuse me, Mr. Taylor. Could I talk to you for a minute?"

He shoved the wad of money into his pants pocket and narrowed his eyes. "What can I do for you, Miss Martin?"

"Please call me Briony. After our midnight chat, I think we're beyond formality. May I call you Alan?"

"I guess." His face was a mask of suspicion, and she didn't blame him. Last time they'd had a conversation, she'd threatened him with a butcher's knife. "I don't have long. I need to get home and wash up," he said, showing her his dirty hands. He smelled of fish, too.

"I understand, but this is important. You'll want to hear what I have to say." Two more men exited the scale house and walked by, staring at her as they passed. "Can we go somewhere more private?" she asked.

Alan led her away from the scale house to a tree that they stood under. "What is it, miss? I'm tired."

Briony wanted to be sensitive, but she had no time to beat around the bush. "Alan, do you believe in the afterlife?"

Stacey Coverstone

His head angled. "If you're talking about life after death, the answer is yes. I believe in going to either Heaven or Hell when we die."

"That's not exactly what I mean." She coughed to clear the emotion in her voice. "Do you believe that spirits can contact us from the other side?"

"Spirits?" His eyes flamed with curiosity, and Briony realized how twinkling green they were. "Have you seen a ghost?" he asked.

"Why, yes! Yes, I have!" This might be easier to explain than she'd thought.

His gaze raked her up and down. "There are ghosts wandering all over Cape Marble, Briony. They're lost souls who are in limbo. They don't understand that they've passed, but they've sinned in this life, so their punishment is to roam through the physical world for all eternity, confused and alone." His eyes assessed her so coolly she shivered under their intensity. "It's what the sinful deserve. I suspect your father is one of them now."

She struggled to tamp down her exasperation. The man's holier than thou attitude fired her blood. Her hot response exploded through her lips before she could stop herself. "Then your sister, Sally, must have been a real peach of a sinner, because I've seen her ghost twice!"

Chapter Seven

Alan's face went pale. His fists pumped at his sides, clutching and unclutching. Briony was prepared to kick him and run if he lashed out at her.

"What kind of sick joke are you trying to pull on me? What do you mean you've seen my sister?"

"If you promise to stay calm, I'll explain the best way I know how," she said. He snorted a gruff promise, and she gave him the abbreviated version of her experience, while leaving out the parts about the crying babies and the blood soaking Sally's dress, out of respect for his loss and what Sally must have suffered.

Alan plowed a hand through his short hair. Apparently speechless, he closed his eyes and said nothing for several long moments.

"Sally's never manifested herself to you?" Briony asked, softly.

His eyes opened, and he shook his head. "No. But she died in the lighthouse. I suppose that's why she's haunting that area. I never go down there. Being at the cottage last night was the closest I've been to the lighthouse since she died."

Briony touched his arm and felt the rigid muscles under her fingertips. "I'm not sure Sally's haunting the lighthouse, Alan. There was nothing frightening about her appearances. And believe me, I've spent most of my life being scared by the least little thing. As you've suggested, I'm not sure she realizes she's passed on. She seemed happy and content."

His broad shoulders sagged with what appeared to be relief. "That's good to know. Why are you telling me all this?"

Briony hadn't been sure until now. "I understand how you've wanted to blame someone—my father—for Sally's death. But I also believe you've unjustly put the burden on him so you wouldn't have to face your own guilt."

Alan's eyes flashed with fury, and she squeezed his arm tighter. "It must have been terribly difficult for you when you found out your little sister was pregnant and had been left alone to deal with her situation."

He gritted his teeth. "She was so young. I had no idea she was messing around. And he was an older guy who took advantage of her."

"Of course you didn't know. Sally made a mistake. It was a huge one, but she came to you for help. You were her big brother, and she trusted you'd know what to do to make things right. You knew her reputation would be ruined if she delivered the baby, so you made a decision. You contacted my father and paid for an abortion."

Alan's head hung on his chest, acknowledging the truth.

"When she died of a hemorrhage, you didn't have the guts to blame yourself, so you blamed my father. He was an easy scapegoat. Isn't that right?"

A low growl escaped Alan's throat.

"Life isn't always fair," Briony continued, "but holding onto the guilt has made you a hostile man. Sally wouldn't want that. I told you about her because I believe, if you know she's at peace and no longer suffering, it might help you to let go of the pain you've been carrying around. Let go of the anger and guilt, Alan, and perhaps Sally can rest in peace."

His gaze fused with hers. They stared into each other's eyes for a long time. "Why did you come to Cape Marble?" he finally asked.

Her story came pouring out in a rush. "My father left our family fifteen years ago. We hadn't heard from him in all these years until he sent for my brother. He'd been a

Cries in the Mist

doctor in Kansas, but in a letter, he wrote that he was the lighthouse keeper on this island. He said a woman named Mira was missing and that he was in danger and needed Ben's help. But Ben died five years ago. I came in his place. But I was too late."

Alan's grimace was far from sympathetic. "Wickie's dead. You can't help him now."

Her nerves rippled beneath her skin. "You're wrong. If I can find out who murdered him, I'll have done what I came to do."

"Why should you bother? He abandoned you and took up with another woman. And he played God with a lot of women's lives."

Alan didn't need to remind her. She'd seen the cottage he'd shared with Mira, and the chamber of horrors in which he conducted his secret business. "It's true. He made mistakes and did some terrible things. But you and others chose to let him play God. And you'll never convince me he was an evil man who set out to hurt people. He probably thought he was doing a service to those women, including your sister. No one had the right to take his life, even if they didn't agree with his practices."

"So, when you're not talking to ghosts, you're playing detective? Is that it?" Alan asked, smugly. "Have you got any suspects on your list yet?"

Briony pinned him with a placid gaze. "As a matter of fact, I do. And you're right up there at the top."

~ * ~

She slipped into the one phone booth in the village and skimmed through the pages of the directory until she came to last names beginning with an L. Her finger moved down the page. Bingo! Jennifer Lee's address was printed next to her phone number. Having no paper or pen to write with since her purse was at the bottom of the Atlantic Ocean, Briony gazed around to make sure no one was watching and

Stacey Coverstone

then ripped out the page. She'd never broken the law before. Smiling, it felt good to do something wicked for a change.

Jennifer's house was located a mere two blocks away. It was a sweet bungalow with dormers and green shutters. A swinging gate and white picket fence surrounding a manicured yard added to the dollhouse effect. A wreath of fake leaves and acorns hung on her front door.

Briony knocked. Knowing nothing about the woman except that she'd had—and could possibly be still carrying on a relationship with the police chief—Briony's half-thought-out plan involved stretching the truth a bit.

She planned to say that while going through her father's things, she'd found a paper with some names written on it, and she'd wondered if it had been his Will that had not been filed at the time of his death. She'd tell Jennifer her name was on the list, and she'd ask her if an attorney had contacted her. Hopefully, that introduction would lead to some revelations that might implicate the police chief in some sort of wrongdoing. Briony still had the niggling feeling that Pemberton was dirty.

After two more raps, she determined no one was home. "I'll just have to try later."

"Can I help you?"

Briony jumped and turned to face a stunning brunette wearing an ankle-length fox coat. In her hands were oven mitts, in which she held a blue cornflower Corningware casserole dish. "Miss Lee?" Briony asked.

The brunette's ruby red lips parted in a smile. "No. I'm Miss Bright. And you are?"

"Briony Martin. I'd shake your hand but I see yours are full."

"Yes, I've brought a casserole to Jennifer. She's at home sick today. She works for my fiancé. And she also happens to be one of my best friends. Your last name is Martin? Where have I heard that name before? You're not a local, are you?"

"No. I'm just visiting."

Cries in the Mist

"I'm not a local either. I moved here from Portland six months ago after my fiancé and I got engaged. We're to be married in the spring."

"How nice. Congratulations."

"Thank you." She glanced at the door. "Did Jennifer not answer when you knocked?"

"No."

"Perhaps she's napping, although I did telephone her a half an hour ago to let her know I'd be bringing lunch over."

"That's kind of you."

"Well, she *is* a very good friend. And Dennis asked me to pamper her. He couldn't get along without Jennifer. She handles everything for him. This is the first sick day she's taken since she started working in his office."

Briony's antennae went up. "Dennis?"

"Dennis Foley. My fiancé. He's the mayor of Cape Marble." Her mouth opened wide, and her dazzling white smile nearly knocked Briony off her feet. Miss Bright's name certainly fit the bubbly and beautiful woman. It was obvious she was as proud as a peacock to be engaged to the mayor.

Foley's name was in the logbook, but the name of the woman he'd paid an abortion for was illegible. As Briony recalled, the procedure had taken place two months ago. Had Miss Bright been the patient, or someone else? Surely, not Jennifer Lee. That would be unbelievable—two pregnancies by two different men. But perhaps not entirely out of the realm of possibility. Things like that happened all the time on *The Guiding Light*, the soap opera that had been a hit on television for the past few years.

With satisfaction, Briony realized she'd started thinking of everyone on Cape Marble as up to no good or suspect of something. This was the way a detective's mind worked. In her job as a court stenographer, she'd heard plenty of testimony from private investigators. Some of it must have rubbed off on her, which she found helpful right now. If she wanted to determine who had killed her father, she'd have to think and act like a gumshoe.

If Dennis Foley had gotten someone other than his fiancée pregnant, he wouldn't want that information to get around. A scandal would end his engagement and possibly his career, too.

"Martin…" Miss Bright said again.

"My father was the keeper of the lighthouse." Briony spit it out, carefully noting the brunette's reaction.

Her happy smile flipped upside down. "Oh. Now I remember. He…died. I'm sorry."

"Thank you."

"Such a terrible tragedy. Do the police know yet who…who…"

"No," Briony interjected. "They thought it had been murder, but apparently, they now think my father committed suicide. But I don't believe it."

Miss Bright's long eyelashes fluttered. "Oh, my. That's really awful. If you think there's anything my fiancé can do to help get to the truth of the matter, please let us know. My name's Colleen, by the way. Dennis's office is located in the town hall."

"I appreciate that."

Both women turned their heads toward the door when it opened. A platinum blonde wearing a fluffy white bathrobe stood inside the screen. "I thought I heard voices," she said, before sneezing.

"Bless you," Colleen said. "I've brought you a casserole."

"That was sweet of you." The blonde pushed open the screen door to let Colleen in. Then her gaze shifted to Briony. "May I help you?"

"Oh, that's Briony Martin," Colleen said. "She's Wickie's daughter, and she's come to…" Her head tilted. "I'm afraid I don't know why she's come to talk to you, Jennifer. She was here when I arrived." She placed the oven mitts on the foyer table and set the casserole dish on top and then stood next to her friend.

Cries in the Mist

Briony noticed the subtle arch of Jennifer's heavily darkened eyebrow. "Pleased to meet you, Miss Lee." She chose to forego shaking her hand to avoid germs. "I'm sorry to bother you, especially when you aren't feeling well. But I'm wondering if I might trouble you for a few moments of your time. I have some information about my father that might be of interest to you. "

Jennifer wiped her nose with a tissue. "I'm really not up to a conversation right now. Besides, I don't see what information would be of interest to me with regard to Wickie. I barely knew him."

With Colleen listening, it was bad timing to say the least. Briony was about to suggest that they meet tomorrow, if Jennifer felt better, when the telephone blared from atop the foyer table.

"Be a dear and answer that for me, would you?" Jennifer asked Colleen. The brunette nodded and lifted the receiver.

Anxious to see how Jennifer would react, Briony decided to quickly, but quietly blurt out what she'd come to say.

Jennifer's mouth gaped. When she snapped it shut again, her gaze narrowed into pinpoints. "Who else is on that list of your father's?" she asked softly.

"Jen, it's Chief of Police Rick Pemberton on the phone," Colleen interrupted. "He claims it's important, but I told him you're sick. Do you want me to take a message?"

Jennifer stared at Briony, her lips grave and her brow troubled. "No. I'll take it." She strode to the phone and turned her back.

Briony's heart began to pound. What a coincidence that the police chief should be calling Jennifer's house at that exact moment! Obviously, she was still his mistress. Again, she sensed Pemberton had people watching her every move. She even turned to see if she could spot anyone hiding in the bushes outside.

She didn't know whether to stay or go. Colleen smiled

at her and then picked up the casserole dish. "I think I'll take this to the kitchen," she whispered before disappearing into another room.

When Jennifer's head jerked over her shoulder, her dubious gaze locked onto Briony. She didn't bother to lower her voice when she confirmed into the phone, "Petite with long brown hair, and wearing a wool cape? Yes, she's here right now."

Perhaps Briony wasn't cut out to be a detective after all. A lump of fear crawled up her throat. "I should be going." Deciding she was playing with fire, she grasped the door handle.

"Wait!" Jennifer shouted.

"Sorry to have bothered you." Briony pushed through the door and ran down the walk and shoved the swinging gate open. When she reached the street, her head ping-ponged in both directions. Turning right would lead her back to the cottage. But left would take her to the pub—and John.

It seemed her feet had minds of their own. In less than ten minutes, she flew through the tavern door and asked the bartender if John was around.

Chapter Eight

Three old men sitting on bar stools cradling mugs of beer gawked at her without shame. The bartender dumped a bag of peanuts into a glass dish on the counter. "Sorry, miss, but he's not upstairs at the moment. He left about thirty minutes ago. Is there anything I can help ya with?"

Darn. She'd really hoped to be able to speak to John. "No, thank you. Have you any idea when he might return, or where I could find him?"

The bartender shook his head. "No idea, miss. But the village isn't that big. I expect you'll find him soon enough if ya poke your nose around."

"Unless he's hound dogging," one of the old men said in a slurred voice. "That's the kind of poke a nice girl like you might not want to stick her nose in." He cackled into his beer, while his companions only shook their heads.

A flush of heat crept up Briony's neck and into her cheeks. She ignored the crude old man and spoke to the bartender again. "Would you please tell Mr. Fletcher I stopped by and that I'd like to see him, if he has time. He knows where to find me."

"Certainly, miss."

As she turned to leave, the same old man loudly said, "Didn't Johnny have a thing for that girl who works at the diner when they were kids?"

"You mean Liz?" one of the other men asked.

Briony's ears perked. Her footsteps halted.

"Yeah, the redhead. Didn't they run off together?" the old man said.

"You got it partly right, Pete," the bartender chimed in. "Don't you remember how it played out?"

Stacey Coverstone

"Remind me," the old man said. "It was a long time ago."

Even while knowing it was rude to eavesdrop, Briony couldn't make her body move. With baited breath, she stood ramrod straight with her hand on the doorknob. There was no way she could leave before hearing this story.

"Johnny and Liz were headed to the mainland to secretly get married the night after John graduated high school," the bartender said. "He'd confided their plans in Ted. As we all know, Ted and John were father and son, but those two were also best friends back then. Ted kept the kids' secret because he didn't think they'd really go through with it. But when he realized they had every intention of leaving the island that night, he informed Liz's old man. Ted had known Dale all his life, and he didn't think it was right for Liz to leave like that, or for John to steal her away without Dale's permission. Dale was livid. He dragged Liz off the ferry in the nick of time and forbade her to ever see John again. She was only sixteen, you see. And it took Ted and two other men to keep Dale from breaking Johnny's skull."

Briony's palms grew wet. She tried to wrap her head around the knowledge that John and the waitress at the diner had been an item. A jolt of jealousy raced through her.

One of the other men took up the story where the bartender had left off. "Johnny was furious at Ted for betraying him and Liz, so he took the ferry out a few days later and stayed away. You know how hotheaded a young man in love can be."

"He came back when Ted died and cried like a baby," the bartender finished. "They wasted a lot of years."

Briony wondered if John regretted the gulf he'd put between himself and his father for something that had happened so long ago. Had his love been so strong for Liz that he'd been unable to forgive his dad even ten years later? That was a long grudge to hold onto. She visualized his rugged face in her mind. The man was unlike anyone she'd

Cries in the Mist

met in her life. He was like a thorn bush that would prick her finger and draw blood if she got too close. Perhaps it was best to get him out of her head now, before her blossoming feelings grew into something that might only hurt her in the end.

She stepped outside and closed the pub door behind her. It was time to go back to the cottage. She'd hoped to come up with some excuse to speak to Dennis Foley, but her brain felt like scrambled eggs. Probably, Miss Bright or Jennifer Lee had warned him of her by this time, anyway. Between her encounters with ghosts and suspicious woman, not to mention hearing the news about John and the redheaded waitress, Briony was exhausted.

As she walked past the diner, she glanced into the large plate glass window. Liz was taking an order at the table next to it. Her gaze lifted, but she didn't smile. In fact, her eyebrows drew together to form a scowl. Briony shivered. Did Liz have some kind of extrasensory perception? Did she know the men at the bar were just talking about her?

Was Liz still harboring feelings for John? Briony wondered. Could it be possible Liz had heard she was acquainted with him and Liz now felt threatened? Did John still care for her? Had they reconnected since he'd returned?

Briony skated past the diner feeling like her head was going to explode.

Across the street, carved into stone above the door of a two-story building were the words *Cape Marble Town Hall*. As she perused the interesting architectural features of the building, the door opened and two men stepped outside. She sucked in a deep breath. *Speak of the Devil*.

John smiled and shook hands with the man, who was as tall as John, but completely opposite in color and build. His frame was thinner, and his reddish-brown hair was cut such that a cascade of long locks swept over one eye. His smile was wide, and his chin tipped up when he chuckled. He was as handsome as a Hollywood actor.

When Colleen Bright stepped through the door and

laced her arm through his, Briony knew she was catching her first glimpse of the mayor—the same man who'd paid for someone's abortion two months ago. He clapped John on the shoulder, and the three of them laughed. From Briony's perspective, Foley played the role of politician with ease and confidence.

What was John doing there acting all buddy-buddy with the man? Making a social call? Had they been friends in school and were catching up after ten years? It seemed likely. But if that were the case, why hadn't John mentioned they were friends when he told her Dennis Foley's name was in her father's record book? At that time, he'd said he didn't know if the man was married or not. Why had he lied to her?

When Colleen leaned into John and kissed him on the cheek, Briony's muscles tensed. The three of them behaved as if they were old chums. John hadn't been home in ten years, so he'd said. Colleen had only just moved to Cape Marble six months ago. The two of them couldn't possibly know each other. Or could they? Her suspicions mounted again.

She maneuvered the cobblestone walk and sloping hill at a steady clip. She was almost to the dock when she heard her name being called. The timbre voice was familiar. Despite her reservations, she stopped and waited for John to catch up.

"Hey." He smiled upon his approach.

"Hello." He gazed as her so intently as to read her most intimate thoughts. His closeness unnerved her.

"What have you been up to?" he asked. "I thought you might have stopped by the pub by now to see me."

"I did. The bartender told me you weren't in. I asked him to tell you I'd stopped by."

"Oh. I didn't get that message yet. I've been out for a while."

She made no reply, and he offered no more about where he'd been—not that it was any of her business. Since it wasn't, she reminded herself.

"Would you have dinner with me tonight?" he asked.

The invitation seemed to come from out of the blue. "At the diner?" It was the only restaurant on the island. Now that she knew of his history with Liz, she wasn't interested in another encounter with the waitress, or in sitting by politely while the two of them reminisced about their past together.

"Yes, unless you want to cook." He grinned, and Briony noticed for the first time a dimple in his cheek.

"I ate breakfast at the diner and it didn't settle well," she fibbed. "But I'd be getting the short end of the stick if I cooked, wouldn't I? Besides, the cottage has only a wood stove, and I'm far from an expert chef on a cook stove. I practically scorched my grilled cheese sandwich earlier today."

"I have an idea," he replied. "I'll ask Skip to make us one of his homemade pizzas, and I'll toss a salad. Then I'll play delivery boy and we can eat together at the cottage. How does that sound?"

"Who's Skip?"

"My barkeep. He makes the most unbelievable pizza crust. I guarantee you'll love it. Do you like pizza?"

"Sure. Who doesn't like pizza?"

"Then it's a date?"

"I guess so." Her response was dispassionate. She hadn't intended to accept, but something about him made it hard to say no.

"Don't get overly excited," he teased. "I might not be able to stand it."

His joking made her smile. She decided to forget about Liz and Dennis Foley, the suspicions John raised in her, and everything else for a few hours and simply enjoy his company tonight. "Six o'clock?"

"I'll be there on the dot."

~ * ~

He was, and the pizza was as delicious as he'd promised.

"Did you read your father's logbook?" he asked, after they'd eaten and moved from the wooden table to the sofa with their cream puff desserts. According to John, Skip was also a fabulous pastry chef.

"Yes. I can't believe how many patients have been to him these past fifteen years. I'm curious as to how he became established here in Cape Marble. It's so isolated. Maybe he closed his eyes and put his finger on a map and wherever it landed, that's where he went."

"I highly doubt it. Maybe he had a friend who lived here."

Briony had considered that angle, but had quickly dismissed it. "I don't think he knew anyone in Maine."

"Excuse me, but you were only eight when he left home. What would you've known about his private life? Obviously, he had secrets."

She frowned, but knew he was right. "I'm wondering if he performed abortions in Kansas and got into trouble, and that's why he left. Maybe he was about to be arrested."

"It seems plausible."

Briony pushed her cream puff aside. "Or maybe he came here solely because of Mira. Perhaps he met her at a medical conference or something like that. Alan Taylor told me she was his assistant." The surgery room in the lighthouse flashed before her like a lightning storm and caused a shudder to course through her.

John refrained from commenting. He crossed one booted foot over his knee and bit into the cream puff.

"My mother claims she got over Dad years ago," Briony continued, "but I know she's always wondered what happened. We all did. I'll have to explain to her that he was murdered and it had something to do with him performing illegal abortions, but I think I'll leave out the part about him being with Mira. I don't want her to hurt any more than she already has. Telling her what I've discovered will be like

Cries in the Mist

ripping a bandage off a wound that hasn't healed, but it'll also bring much-needed closure. It does for me, sort of. I'm mad that his killer got away with it."

"You don't know he or she will get away with it," John said.

"Yes, I do! The police chief has all but officially closed the case. He now claims Dad committed suicide. That's a bunch of baloney, but I'll never be able to prove it. I need to figure out who the murderer is and get them to confess. I won't be able to rest until I do."

John chuckled. "Good luck with that. The confession part, I mean. Rarely do criminals confess to their crimes."

Briony gritted her teeth. "So now you're an expert in criminals? This isn't a joking matter, John." She wondered again if he had firsthand knowledge.

He uncrossed his leg and leaned toward her. His voice was low, and his eyes burned on her face. "I know, Briony. But you're not a detective. You're going to get hurt if you go around pretending to be. Have faith that the person who killed your father will screw up somehow and lead the law to them. Give it a little time."

She remembered the veiled threat she'd received from Rick Pemberton and Liz's suggestion that she leave the island or end up in a grave next to her father. "I don't have time. I'm leaving Cape Marble in two days when the ferry returns."

Blurting that out surprised even her. On one hand, she wanted to find her father's killer. On the other, John was right. She was a stenographer, not a detective. Her promise to her father would more than likely have to be broken. Chasing criminals was for risk-taking, thrill-seeking people. She was neither. At least, that was her excuse.

"Is your mother wiring you some money for the fare?" John asked.

"No. I have a pair of binoculars I hope to sell. Surely they're worth some money."

His hand covered hers. "Don't leave so soon. We're

just getting to know each other."

She breathed in his intoxicating scent. He was the real reason she needed to leave—and soon. Without fully realizing it, since the age of eight she'd colored every man in her life, with the exception of Ben, with the stain of betrayal. She couldn't risk falling for a guy like John only to have him leave her like his father had left her mother. She and John came from different worlds. It would never work.

Their gazes welded, and his finger made a trail from her jawline to the pulse-beating hollow of her throat. Goose pimples peppered her skin.

"No..." Her soft moan was cut off when his mouth covered hers. Sizzling with desire, Briony pressed into the solid warmth of his chest and answered his kiss.

Chapter Nine

"I can't do this." She broke the kiss and pushed away from him.

"Don't be afraid," John said, threading his fingers through her hair.

"Please, don't." Briony sprung up from the sofa and paced the room. With desperation leaking from her pores, she wanted to pretend the kiss had never happened. Abruptly, she changed the subject. "I've thought about it, and I believe my father's killer must be either Rick Pemberton, his wife Violet, Dennis Foley, Alan Taylor, or Jennifer Lee. They all have good motives. But I can hardly request the police chief to investigate himself, can I?"

Her tongue moved over her bottom lip; the taste of him lingering and causing her to want more. What had he done to her?

With a burst of energy, she revealed to him in a flurry her experiences with Sally, discovering the surgery room in the lighthouse, hearing the crying babies, and seeing the woman in a blue dress. Then she admitted knowing about his past relationship with Liz.

John stared at her for what seemed an eternity.

"Aren't you going to say anything?" she finally asked.

He shrugged his broad shoulders. "I'm not sure what you expect me to say. Hearing about your paranormal experiences comes as no surprise. I told you there were ghosts on this island. As for Liz and me, I have no idea how you got that information, but the relationship ended ten years ago. It's of no consequence."

"But you wanted to marry her."

"Yeah, I did. I was an eighteen-year-old kid. I fell in

love and let my hormones rule my head. I made some mistakes. That's what kids do. You must have fallen for one or two guys when you were that age and then realized they were all wrong for you."

Briony's gaze dropped to the floor. She'd never been in love before.

John ran a hand through his pompadour. "Since I've been away, I haven't been in contact with Liz at all until I came back to bury my old man three weeks ago. Then it was just to say hi when I ran into her at the diner. We grew up together. It didn't work out for us, but I'll always consider her a friend."

Briony cleared her throat. "She told me there are secrets here in Cape Marble that people want to keep hidden. And when I passed by the diner window earlier today, she glared at me, like she wanted to rip my throat out. I got the feeling she knew you and I were acquainted and she's jealous."

John shook his head. "That's not true, Briony. I know for a fact that Liz was in a relationship until recently. The scumbag used her and then left the island."

"What do you mean he used her?"

A rush of air expelled from John's mouth. "He knocked her up and then left her high and dry. Sorry to be so blunt."

"How do you know that? Did Liz tell you?"

"No. Dennis Foley did. He and Liz have been friends all their lives. They lived next door to each other as children."

Briony's eyes enlarged. "Did the mayor share that information about Liz today when you visited him at the town hall?"

John's gaze narrowed. "How do you know I was at the town hall?"

There was no point in her avoiding the truth. "I was across the street and saw you speaking to him outside. I assumed you saw me, too, since you followed me to the

Cries in the Mist

dock. Do you also know his fiancée, Colleen Bright?"

"Today was the first time I'd met her. She showed up just as we finished our talk and were exiting his office."

"She kissed you on the cheek."

John's mouth tipped. "I think that's the kind of girl she is. Touchy-feely."

Briony was more direct when she rephrased her question with regard to Dennis and Liz. "When Dennis told you Liz got pregnant by this so-called scumbag, did he also admit to her having gotten an abortion?"

John appeared surprised. "How did you know?"

Exhilaration spirited through her. She ran to the brass bed and stuck her hand underneath the mattress and pulled out the record book. After plopping back onto the sofa and flipping to the page with Dennis's name, she pointed to the illegible smudge. "I assumed the mayor got someone pregnant and didn't want his fiancée to find out. Do you think it was Liz he got pregnant, and he's covering by telling you it was some guy who left the island?"

"You're starting to think like a cop," John said, grinning. "It's a good guess, but unfortunately, it's a wrong guess."

Briony's mouth turned down, and she sighed.

"Dennis didn't get Liz pregnant. That would almost be incest, as close as they are. But he *did* pay for her abortion." He tapped the smudge with his finger. "Liz *was* your father's patient. She's twenty-six years old and still scared of what her dad is going to think. When she found out she was in trouble, she went to Dennis for help. He's always been there for her. He agreed to pay for the abortion and keep her secret quiet. That's why his name is in the book."

Briony thought about that for a moment. Something didn't make sense. "You and Dennis Foley haven't seen each other in years, you said. This is not a topic that just happened to come up in casual conversation today. Why did you really go to see him, John?"

His faraway expression changed to sharp awareness

that made her heartbeat race. "I can't tell you, Briony. Not yet."

"Not yet? Then when?" Her voice shook with emotion. She hated secrets!

"Soon, I hope. I'm asking you to trust me on this."

Trust him? How could she trust a man she barely knew? John—an enigma—held grudges and hid secrets of his own. Why was she bothering to talk to him about this, anyway? It made no difference to him who her father's murderer was.

She slammed the cover on the logbook shut. "I don't care about Liz or Dennis Foley, unless one of them murdered my father. Is one of them my father's murderer? If you know the answer to that question, I want you to tell me right now!"

He laced his fingers together and quietly replied. "I don't know."

Frustrated, she hurled the logbook at the wood stove. It bounced off the iron side and then landed on the floor with a thud. "This conversation is over," she announced.

When John made no attempt to appease her ruffled feathers, she squeezed back tears that threatened to burst from her eyes. He said goodbye and showed himself to the door. It clicked shut, and the ache she felt in her chest turned to a deep, agonizing burn.

Sometime later, she stepped outside and gazed at the moon. Its golden glow lit the path leading to the lighthouse, making the shells look more like twinkling diamonds than broken seashells. Briony stared at the dark tower beyond. A cool breeze whipped her hair around her face. She hugged her body tight as needles of awareness pricked her skin.

She sniffed. The air around her didn't smell like rain. It smelled of perfume—the same scent she'd smelled in the cottage and on the stairs of the lighthouse.

As if on cue, the lamp in the tower flickered on. Briony stood motionless with her breath locked deep inside her throat. The figure of a woman floated along the observation deck. Although the light from the lens shown through her transparent body, it was clear that she wore a long blue dress.

"Mira, is it you?" Briony whispered.

She blinked. When her eyes opened, the woman was gone.

~ * ~

She woke the next morning groggy and confused. The mists of a gloomy autumn morning filtered through the dirty window, their eerie shadows splashing onto the cottage walls. Briony snuggled further into the heat of the soft blankets and ignored the intrusion into her warm cocoon.

A pounding on the door sent her body shooting upright. She rubbed her knuckles over her eyes wondering if she'd been dreaming. The sound of footsteps running over the gravel path outside assured her she wasn't. She scampered off the bed. The floor was cold on her bare feet when she scurried across it.

She turned the latch on the door, but it wasn't locked! How stupid she'd been. She must have fallen asleep last night without securing the bolt. When she opened the door and stepped onto the stoop, she looked in both directions, but saw no one coming or going.

Her head turned. A note was nailed to the door. A tingle moved across her shoulders as she removed the paper from the nail head. In an instant, she realized the risk someone had taken in order to hammer the nail into the door so early in the morning with her sleeping inside.

Her gaze darted all around again, and then she scrambled into the cottage and bolted the lock. Her back pressed against the wood. The paper on which the words were typed was white and nondescript. The note read:

Stacey Coverstone

> I KNOW WHO KILLED WICKIE.
> I WAS A WITNESS BUT AM AFRAID.
> MEET ME IN THE LIGHTHOUSE AT 8 P.M. TONIGHT.
> BRING THE LOGBOOK WITH YOU.

Briony couldn't believe her eyes. Someone was willing to come forward and help her! Granted, the clandestine method of communication bordered on the melodramatic, but as long as the outcome was met, it didn't matter if the note had been scribbled on a napkin. The important thing was that she'd be able to keep her promise to her father and go back to Kansas with an unburdened conscience.

The hours couldn't tick by fast enough. Having no desire to run into anyone in the village, and especially John, she spent part of the morning in the cottage trying to read one of the books found on the bookshelf. With her mind wandering and unable to stay on track, she ate an apple and then walked to the dock and sat on a bench near the shore.

Being on or in the water still frightened her and reminded her of Ben's tragic demise. But to experience the ocean from a safe distance would be a good first step toward healing. If she could learn to appreciate it for its power and magnificence rather than think of it as her brother's watery tomb, she might make some headway on tackling that particular fear. Making the journey from Kansas to Maine on her own had bolstered her courage. The things she'd experienced in two days on Cape Marble only added to her determination to eradicate all her fears and anxieties. It might take some time, but she felt her confidence building.

When she noticed Alan Taylor climbing out of his fishing boat, she turned her head, hoping he didn't notice her. A few minutes later, he plopped onto the bench. The stench of fish permeating from his body nearly made her gag.

"Afternoon, Briony."

She met his gaze. "Good afternoon, Alan. Is your work day over already?"

Cries in the Mist

He pulled a hankie out of the pocket of his slicker and cleaned his hands. "There's a problem with my cooler, so I had to come in early."

"I hope it doesn't take long for it to be repaired. Fishing is your livelihood, is it not?"

He nodded and then followed her gaze to the water. "Are you enjoying the view?"

"Yes, it's a pleasant day. The waves don't seem too rough." *Enough with the small talk*, she thought. "I don't think you walked over here to chit-chat. What's on your mind, Alan?"

A sheepish expression filled his wind-burned face. "I want to apologize for scaring you at the cottage that night, and also for being rude to you yesterday when you told me about Sally."

"Apology accepted." Briony hoped to end the conversation as quickly as possible. Her mind was on her meeting tonight with the mystery note writer. And he'd interrupted her practice of deep breathing that helped calm her.

"Just like that?" he asked, looking amazed.

"Just like that. Life is too short to hold grudges."

Alan's mouth tipped up at the corners. "You're right, Briony. I'll try to remember that from now on."

She returned a small smile.

He cleared his throat. "She came to me last night."

Briony's head jerked back to him. "Sally?"

"Yes. She told me she's at peace, and she asked me to let go of my bitterness. She said she's unable to go into the light and cross over until I do."

"Are you willing to do that for her?"

"She's my baby sister. I'd do anything for her."

Briony patted his arm. Her gaze delved into him, and something hinted he wasn't a killer. His eyes no longer crackled with fury. The irises sparkled as blue-green as the rippling sea that he sailed on every day. Mentally, she erased him from her list of suspects.

He stood up and offered his hand. Despite the fishy smell, she shook it. "Good luck, Alan."

"Same to you, Briony. I hope justice is served someday."

She knew what he meant; that her father's murderer would be caught. "Thank you." Even Alan's walk seemed more relaxed as he returned to his boat.

Although she hadn't wanted to go into the village, when her stomach growled, she realized she'd barely eaten since arriving on Cape Marble. She decided to make a quick trip to the market.

By the time she exited with some salad fixings and a can of tomato soup she planned to heat on the wood stove, the temperature outside had significantly dropped.

She pulled her cape tight and clutched at the paper sack in her hand. As she carefully treaded down the cobblestone walk toward the hill, a flash of movement from across the street caught in the corner of her eye. A strange sensation washed over her. She glanced around. Someone ducked behind the corner of a building next to the town hall and hid in the shadows. A chill crept over Briony's nape.

Who was trailing her? The Chief of Police? Or someone else?

Chapter Ten

With the undeniable feeling that someone was stalking her, Briony hurried to the cottage, peeking over her shoulder every few seconds, with her heart galloping. Once she was safely locked inside, she spent the next thirty minutes hiding behind the window casing and sneaking glances out the glass. No shadows crept into view. No footsteps shuffled outside the door. No ghosts appeared.

When she'd successfully reined in her fear using her deep breathing techniques, she ate dinner, washed the dishes, and then tried to read again. When that failed, she fed the wood stove a few more logs and then stretched her frame upon the sofa and waited for time to pass. The wind outside howled like a coyote, but inside the little house, it was as warm as toast.

At some point, she drifted off to sleep. The patter of rain on the roof stirred her awake, and she rubbed a crick out of her neck. The lumpy sofa was far from comfortable for a long nap. She glanced out the window and saw only darkness. Jolting upright, she read the time on her watch: seven-fifty.

The inside of her mouth turned as dry as sawdust. It was time to meet the witness to her father's murder at the lighthouse. Thank God she hadn't overslept! She jumped up from the sofa and scurried about the room, feeling excited and scared at the same time. She wasn't particularly looking forward to entering the tower after yesterday's peculiar events.

The note had said to bring the logbook with her. She hadn't questioned that request until now. But there was no time to ponder. She wrapped up in her cape, stuck the logbook inside the interior pocket to keep it dry, and grabbed a flashlight from off the kitchen counter. Unfortunately, she could locate no umbrella.

Adrenaline rushed through her veins as she shut the cottage door behind her and scurried down the seashell path to the lighthouse. Just as she reached the tower, a great clap of thunder startled her. Her gaze lifted upward to the lantern room. The lamp wasn't on, and she saw no sign of another flashlight moving around inside. Was she the first to arrive?

Rain dripped from her hair and spilled down her face. She couldn't stand here or she'd catch her death of pneumonia.

Briony pushed open the door and stepped into the cold, dark entry. A clang reverberated throughout the room when the metal door closed behind her, causing her to flinch.

"Hello? Is anyone here?" She swung her flashlight around, shining its narrow beam into the corners of the circular room, seeking out shadows. As her eyes adjusted to the murky interior, a rustling sound came from around the corner in the direction of the surgery chamber. The memory of the crying babies and the heaviness she'd felt inside that room caused her muscles to tense.

"Who's there?" With her feet frozen to the ground, she pointed the flashlight in that direction. Her heart beat so fast and hard she swore it might burst from her chest. A whistle of air whooshed from her lips when a mouse squeaked and ran up the hall and into a crack in the wall.

"Get a hold of yourself," she said out loud. "It was just a mouse." She moved the flashlight's beam toward the spiral staircase. "Hello? It's Briony Martin. Is anyone here?" she repeated.

"Upstairs," replied a voice. It was a woman's voice, and it came from the lantern room.

Briony's gaze lifted. A soft groan tore from her throat when she glimpsed a white face staring at her from the stairwell above. As quickly as it appeared, it disappeared back into the gloom.

Cries in the Mist

She'd seen a face staring at her yesterday, too. Could it be Mira who'd summoned her, after all? Briony had almost convinced herself that Mira was a spirit who haunted the lighthouse. Now she believed her father's mistress was as flesh and blood as she was. She must have been hiding in the lighthouse all this time, afraid, because she'd seen who'd murdered her Wickie.

Suddenly, Briony's fear dissolved like mist. She wasn't afraid of Mira. Hopefully, the woman would confide in her as she'd promised in the note, and they'd be able to set things straight with the police. If Rick Pemberton was involved, Briony would go to the law on the mainland.

"Hurry," whispered the voice.

"I'm coming." Briony started the climb. The metal rungs of the stairs echoed with every footstep. Above her, she heard the sound of pacing. When she reached the lantern room, she moved the flashlight around. There was no one there.

"Out here," said the voice. It came from the observation deck.

Briony slowly made her way around the giant lamp to the opening that led onto the deck. When she stepped outside, cold wind blasted straight through her. Fortunately, the rain had all but stopped, but gray mist clung heavily around her like a wet blanket.

One hundred feet below, waves pounded violently upon what Briony knew were jagged rocks. Her head swam with a dizzying nausea. She grasped the iron rail and held on for dear life when she realized nothing stood between her and certain death but a metal grate floor.

"Did you bring the logbook?" asked the woman, who stood about twelve feet away with her back to Briony.

"Yes."

"Come closer and lay it down near my feet."

Briony took a few wobbly steps while sliding her hand along the rail. She stopped, caught her breath, and studied the woman's figure through the mist. If it was Mira, she'd expected to find her in a coat because of the foul weather, but with the long blue dress peeking out from underneath. That's what she'd seen her in twice. Instead, she wore woolen trousers, boots, and what appeared to be a man's jacket. Her hair was tucked inside a fedora hat. Were they her father's clothes?

"Why do you need the record book?" Briony asked, clutching it tightly inside the cape. A niggling feeling told her something wasn't right.

"Don't ask questions. Just give it to me!" cried the woman.

"Are you Mira?"

The woman's shoulders grew rigid. She mumbled something under her breath. Then suddenly, she whirled. The mist parted, and Briony could see her mouth was twisted into an ugly grin. "Mira's dead," she gritted.

The face was vaguely familiar. The men's clothing confused Briony, but the woman's skin was as smooth as porcelain. And her face was as beautiful as a model's. Where had she seen her before?

Flashbacks came to her in a rush. She gasped. "You're Colleen Bright!" But why was she wearing men's clothes and demanding she hand over her father's logbook? Briony's mind swirled with questions.

"That's right. Now hand over the record book, unless you want to end up like Mira."

She felt her stomach sink like a stone. When she hesitated, Colleen screamed, "Hand over Wickie's book!" She withdrew a revolver from the pocket of her jacket and aimed. Briony pulled the book from inside her cape and tossed it on the floor in front of her.

Colleen's eyes widened. "You idiot! It could have slipped through the cracks!" With the gun trained on Briony, she darted forward and grabbed the book and then backed up again.

"I don't understand," Briony said. Her mind began to work, trying to figure out how she could drop and roll

Cries in the Mist

through the opening and run down the spiral staircase before Colleen could get a shot off. "What happened to Mira?"

Colleen waved the gun toward the railing. "She had a little accident. I'd intended on confronting Wickie about the little matter of him performing illegal abortions, but he wasn't at the cottage that day. I saw Mira in her long dress and orthopedic shoes limping down the path to the lighthouse, so I followed her. I found her out here on the observation deck. I knew Wickie kept records on who'd had abortions and who'd paid for them. She wouldn't tell me where his book was. I tried to reason with her, but she was very uncooperative. Unfortunately, she slipped and fell over this railing."

It hadn't been an accident at all. Shuddering, Briony closed her eyes and imagined the screams as Mira plummeted to her death. Her body must have washed out to sea, which is why she'd never been found.

Her eyes opened. Colleen stared over the railing in a trance-like state. She was probably recalling that day. Briony quietly backed up a few steps hoping this was her chance to escape.

"Don't try anything funny," Colleen warned, snapping back to reality. She waved the revolver in the air. Briony halted her steps, but felt she had nothing to lose. If she was going to die, she wanted to know the truth of what had happened to her father.

"How did you know my father kept a logbook of the surgeries he performed?"

Colleen spit out her response. "I overheard Dennis talking on the phone. I realized he'd gotten someone pregnant. The bastard! We're to be married in the spring, and he'd knocked up another woman! Something Dennis said in his phone conversation led me to believe Wickie kept a record of who got abortions and who paid for them. Can you imagine what a scandal that would cause if word leaked out that Dennis was involved in such unsavory activities? It would ruin his reputation, and the people would run him out of office. I couldn't let that happen. I'm going to be the mayor's wife, damn it!"

She flipped the fedora off her head, and her long black hair tumbled out and down her back. "I've waited all my life to become the wife of a rich and powerful man. I wasn't about to let anything stand in my way. I'm still not. And I mean nothing!"

Although Dennis Foley hadn't cheated, Colleen apparently didn't care if he had. All she'd been concerned about was her social status in the community. Briony shook her head, disgusted. "What about my father? I assume you murdered him, too?"

Colleen sighed. "I liked Wickie. I really did. I hated to do it, but he was just as stubborn as his gimpy wife. It took several visits to get him alone, but when I finally did, he refused to acknowledge that he kept any records." She laughed, but there was a false note in her mirth. "He lied! I had to kill him so I could search his cottage for the evidence." Her lips pursed. "I looked high and low, but the book wasn't to be found. I've been stewing for weeks now. I didn't know what to do. And then *you* came to the island." She smiled. "When I heard you tell Jennifer that you'd found a notebook with some names in it, I *knew* it was Wickie's records. I could see straight through you."

Briony shrugged. "I'm not a good liar."

"So you see why I had to trick you into coming here and handing over the logbook. Now Dennis and I can get married and everything will be all right. No one has to know what he did." She cocked the revolver. "I'm sorry we didn't get to know each other better, Miss Martin. We might have been friends in different circumstances."

"Wait! You don't want to do this," Briony said, creeping away from the railing. "Dennis didn't even get anyone pregnant. He paid for an abortion for a friend. You killed my father and Mira for no reason. Maybe you can plead guilty by insanity and the court will be merciful."

"What?" Colleen's hand lowered. Her eyebrows drew

together. "Dennis didn't impregnate anyone?"

"No. He loves you. He was only helping out a friend. There won't be any scandal. No one has to know anything."

Colleen's head tilted. "Mmmm. That's interesting. But you still know what I did to Wickie and Mira." She lifted the gun again. "I'm sorry, Briony, but you must be silenced."

Chapter Eleven

"Briony! Briony!"

Someone banged on the lighthouse door shouting her name. She'd recognize that deep voice anywhere. "John!" she screamed over the rail. "Up here! She has a gun!"

"Shut up," Colleen cried. The hand holding the gun shook. She fiercely clutched the logbook with the other. "I have to kill you. You know that."

"No. You don't want more blood on your hands, Colleen. If you shoot me, you'll have to shoot John, too. That'll be four murders. You'll never become the mayor's wife. Murder is frowned upon in polite society, you know."

Briony slowly inched forward, hoping the fog would roll in again. That would give her an opportunity to rush Colleen and bat the gun from her hand. If that didn't work, she'd try to distract her with babble long enough for John to come to her aid. Why wasn't he up here already? She heard a few more pounds on the door downstairs. It must have locked itself when it slammed shut.

"I have no choice," Colleen said, coldly. "I'll dump both of your bodies over the rail like I did with Mira. The police will think you had a lover's quarrel and there was a struggle and an accident."

Colleen's finger thumbed the trigger and the gun exploded, but the shot went wild. Briony dove to the grate floor and instinctively covered her head with her hands. Her last thought—because she knew she was about to die—was, *I'm coming home, Ben.*

When she heard Colleen's boots thud toward her, she lifted her head and gazed into her eyes. If she was going to die, she wanted her murderer to forever be haunted by the memory of her face. Colleen splayed her legs apart and cocked the revolver again.

Suddenly, the thunderous roar of crying babies arose from out of nowhere. Their mournful cries sounded like the combination of a flock of seagulls squawking and a tidal wave hitting the shore. Briony stumbled to her feet and covered her ears. The logbook slipped out of Colleen's hands, and she lowered the gun.

"What's happening?" she screamed.

The gigantic lamp flickered on, and a blast of cold air blew out from the lantern room. It chilled Briony's body to the bone. She staggered to the railing and gripped it tight. Her eyes popped open when a phantom in a long blue dress soared out of the room through the opening with her arms spread like the wings of a bird. Briony could see straight through her transparent body. The specter's eyes blazed with fire and fury. Her hands were curled like claws with fingernails as sharp as talons. She flew by Briony without a glance and rocketed toward Colleen with her arms outstretched. Her hair fanned wildly around her head. A shriek as horrifying as a banshee's burst from her mouth.

Colleen's gun clattered to the grate floor. Her face petrified into an expression of terrified surprise. Briony's mouth gaped as Colleen stumbled backwards. Her feet lifted off the ground, her back arched, and her body slipped over the rail.

Later, when the shock had ebbed, Briony would realize she hadn't even heard Colleen scream.

Briony slammed her eyes shut. When they finally opened again, she was huddled in a ball on the grate floor. The only sound she heard was the crashing of the waves far below. She lifted her head and rocked to her knees.

The woman in blue was gone, but tiny particles resembling snow began to shimmer within a shaft of moonlight in front of her. Within moments, the particles had morphed into the figure of a man. Briony's hand covered her mouth. "Father!"

Stacey Coverstone

His voice sounded far far away when he spoke. "I'm sorry, Briony. I loved you and your brother, and your mother, too. I made mistakes. Please forgive me."

She removed her hand from her mouth, and tears sprang into her eyes. "I love you, too," she whispered. They stood looking at one another for what seemed an eternity. Then he smiled and nodded, blew her a kiss, and disappeared.

Heavy footfalls pounded up the spiral staircase. Two strong hands grasped her by the shoulders and hauled her to her feet. John's arms surrounded her. She placed her head on his chest, and he stroked her hair, whispering into her neck, "Everything's all right now. I'm here."

~ * ~

Back at the cottage, while Briony was in the bathroom changing into dry clothes, she heard John call Rick Pemberton on the rotary telephone and tell him Colleen Bright was dead. After a brief conversation, he hung up the phone. She came out of the bathroom, slid onto the rocking chair, and watched him silently putter around.

He stoked the fire. Then he heated coffee on the wood stove. When it was ready, he filled two mugs and handed her one. After covering her legs with a blanket, he settled into the cushions on the sofa. He took a sip of his coffee. Then he explained everything.

"It's true that my old man and I had a falling out when I was a kid. I had a hot head at that age. But I forgave him years ago. I don't get back to the island often because of my job, but he and I have stayed in touch. He contacted me three weeks ago asking for help. He said a good friend of his had been murdered, and he didn't trust the police chief to solve the case. In fact, he thought Rick Pemberton might have been involved somehow. Pop also said that his friend's wife was missing."

Briony nibbled her lower lip. "His friend was my dad,

Cries in the Mist

and Mira was the missing woman."

"Yeah. Pop thought I could help because I'm a private detective."

Briony's eyes enlarged with surprise. "You are? And you work on the mainland?" That explained his comment about knowing his way around the court system.

"Yes. I've been a P.I. for five years now. When Pop called me a few weeks ago, he told me about your father, Hugh Martin. They'd become fast friends when they both attended a summer camp here in Maine back when they were in high school. They never lost touch with one another."

Her mouth dropped open. "I had no idea my father had ever traveled east, even when he was growing up. He never mentioned Maine, as far as I can remember."

John continued. "When you suspected he'd been performing abortions in Kansas, you were right. Something tragic happened to a patient, and the girl's family caused a stink. He was afraid of being arrested. That's how he ended up here in Cape Marble." His gaze delved deep into her eyes. "Do you want me to keep going?"

"Of course. I can take it. I need to hear the truth, all of it."

"According to my old man, your father chose to run away instead of face the music, as they say. He contacted Pop, knowing we lived far away from civilization, and arrangements were made. It so happened the lighthouse keeper at the time was ready to retire, so Pop arranged for your father to take over the job. No one would ever have to know what had happened in Kansas, and your father could start a new life here as Wickie. Unfortunately, the plan also meant leaving you, your brother, and your mother behind." He paused. "Now comes the part as to why he cut off all ties with your family."

After seeing her father's spirit on the observation deck, her resolve to forgive hadn't vacillated, but could she ever forget what he'd done? She'd waited too long not to hear all the facts. "What was it?"

"According to Pop, your father considered bringing you all with him. But he didn't want to uproot your lives and make you all accomplices to his crimes. It would be too hard to explain to you and your brother why you had to leave all your friends and move across country to this isolated place. Plus, he didn't think your mother would ever forgive him for performing abortions, because of her religious convictions. That's why he ultimately left without a word."

She frowned. "He could have written Ben and I at some point, and at least let us all know he wasn't dead."

"He wanted to protect your family."

"How was not contacting us protecting us?"

"Think about it, Briony. When the family of that patient filed a lawsuit and your father couldn't be found, the police would have questioned your mother. They probably did, but you were too young to know. If she legitimately didn't know anything about his illegal practices and could also say in good conscience that she had no idea where he'd fled, they wouldn't have a leg to stand on. Eventually they'd have to close their investigation. No one from Kansas would imagine looking for him in faraway Maine on some isolated island. The trail would grow cold and he'd be out of the woods, so to speak, which seems to be what happened."

"Until he took up performing abortions here and his illegal activities finally caught up with him."

John nodded. "He probably could have continued for years. Seemed he had quite an underground business going on. And from what Pop told me, Wickie thought he was doing a good service to those women."

She sighed, confused as to her stance on the position.

"Briony, it's probably of little consolation, but, according to Pop, your father did have your family's best interests in mind when he left the way he did. He always missed you. And he never stopped loving you."

She mulled that over. He may have missed them, but that didn't make him any less of a coward. His decision to steal away in the night and leave Kansas rather than face the consequences of his actions caused them all so much pain. But she'd promised to forgive him. His way of thinking at the time probably made sense to him. She had no intentions of growing old with a bitter heart. And she wanted him to rest in peace.

"If he came here fifteen years ago," she said, "you knew him. What did your dad tell you about my father when he arrived?"

"I only knew he was an old friend, that was it. I was thirteen and interested in girls and sports. I didn't care who the light keeper was, or where he'd come from."

"Do you remember when he took up with Mira?"

"I'm not sure. It must have been sometime after I left the island."

Her mind went back to what John had told her the day they met. "When we talked on the ferry, why did you tell me you hadn't seen or spoke to your father in ten years? I now know that was an outright lie."

"As soon as you introduced yourself, I realized you were Hugh's daughter. I was shocked. Pop had no idea he'd written to your brother. When you told me you'd come in your brother's place to help out your father…"

"You knew he was already dead."

"Yes, but I couldn't tell you. It was crucial that no one knew I was coming back to Cape Marble to conduct my own undercover investigation into Wickie's murder. I'd just buried Pop three weeks before. I couldn't devote my time to this case until I'd tied one up at home, so I went back to the mainland. Cleaning out Pop's apartment and settling his estate was a good cover for me to return, but it was also the truth. I'm sorry I couldn't tell you everything then, but I couldn't blow my cover. I wasn't sure if I could trust anyone here."

"How did your dad die?" she asked.

"Of a brain aneurism. Skip found him upstairs. The doctor said Pop didn't suffer. He literally didn't know what hit him."

"I'm sorry."

"Thanks. My mom passed away when I was six. My old man and me, all we had was each other. I regret wasting even that short time being angry with him when I was a younger man."

"It's in the past now. You made your peace before it was too late. That was the most important thing."

He nodded. "That's the reason I wanted to solve your father's murder. Pop wanted justice to be served. Wickie was his good friend. I'd like to think my old man is looking down on us happy that we caught the perpetrator."

Briony smiled. "I'm sure he is." Her gaze moved to the kitchen table where her father's record book lay. "Why do you suppose that book was in your dad's trunk in his closet?"

John shrugged. "All I can figure is that after Mira turned up missing, Wickie knew he was in danger, too. He must have trusted my pop with it for safekeeping. He hadn't mentioned the notebook to me when he first called. Then he died before we talked again."

Briony had one more question to ask. "How did you know I was at the lighthouse tonight and in trouble?"

"I've been subtly interviewing those who I considered suspects—the same as you, I came to learn—and my suspicions rested on Violet Pemberton at first. It's usually the real quiet ones you have to watch. They hold everything in until one day—he clicked his fingers—they snap, and that's all she wrote."

"I thought it was her, too!"

They laughed together and then his face sobered. "I was following you earlier today. Did you sense me?"

She straightened her back. "Yes! I saw someone fall into the shadows beside the town hall. I thought it was the police chief or one of his deputies."

"It was me. I knew you'd been making inquiries about town, so I wanted to keep an eye on you. I wasn't kidding

Cries in the Mist

when I said Mainers don't like people snooping in their business. I wouldn't be able to forgive myself if something happened to you."

Their gazes fused, and Briony felt heat creep into her cheeks.

"Anyway, while I was still hiding behind that corner, a woman in a trench coat walked by me. At first, I thought it was Violet Pemberton. Then I realized it was Dennis's fiancée. I assumed she'd just come from seeing Dennis. Her high heel got stuck in a crack between the cobblestones. She swore under her breath when wriggling her foot didn't loosen the heel. When she bent down to pull the heel out of the crack, I glimpsed the butt of a gun poking up from her coat pocket. All kinds of red flags began waving. I followed her home and then kept surveillance outside her house the rest of the evening. Around seven-fifty, she exited her house wearing men's clothes. I almost didn't know it was her at first. I thought it was Dennis."

"Her plan must have been not to be recognized as a woman if someone saw her coming to the lighthouse."

John continued. "I stayed a safe distance behind and trailed her here to the cottage. Then I heard a strange moaning sound coming from the weeds."

Briony wondered if it had been Sally Taylor, or another ghost.

"An old man had fallen and hurt his leg," John said. "He was without a coat and shaking. I couldn't just leave him alone in the cold and dark with a bum leg."

"Of course not."

"I hauled him up the hill and asked someone in the diner to phone the doctor. Then I ran back here as fast as I could." His mouth formed a thin line. "I should have left the old man. You could have been killed."

That was a fact, but he hadn't saved her, anyway. Mira and the babies had. And she'd looked death in the eyes and not felt fear, which made her proud.

Briony leaned forward and patted his hand. "We're

both alive, and my father's murderer was caught. That's all that matters, although I would have liked for her to be tried and sentenced for her crime. It sounds mean, but I would have preferred Miss Bright suffer in prison the rest of her life."

"There's not a mean bone in your body," John said.

She smiled. "You might change your mind if you get to know me better, but I do intend to live the rest of my life without regrets and not holding onto grudges."

"That's a good philosophy." He angled his head. "You haven't yet told me how Colleen fell over the railing. Did she slip?"

That part of the story would take too much energy to explain. Hopefully, he'd believe her account of the supernatural events that had taken place, when she decided to share them. "I'm so tired right now. Can we talk about that later?" she asked.

"Sure. Rick Pemberton plans to start the search for her body tomorrow. It's too late tonight. He said he'd give Dennis the bad news."

Briony nodded, wondering if the sea might finally give up Mira's body, too. If she was ever to be found, Briony wanted her to be buried next to her Wickie.

Chapter Twelve

Briony stood on the dock watching the approach of the ferry that would take her back to the mainland. From there, she'd ride a bus and then the train home to Kansas. She hadn't had to sell her father's binoculars, after all. John had loaned her the money for the fares.

He stood next to her wearing the same pea coat she'd first seen him in, with her suitcase at his feet.

"Thank you again for the loan," she said. I promise to repay you every penny. I'll send the money to you in three installments; the first one starting with my next paycheck."

He grinned. "I trust you, Briony, and there's no hurry. I'll look forward to receiving mail from you. I hope you'll send a letter along with each payment. You didn't lose my address, did you?"

"No." She patted the big bag hanging on her shoulder. "It's inside here. As soon as I get home, I'm going to buy a new purse and address book, and your name will be the first one I write in."

With his fingers, he thumped his chest where his heart beat. "I feel honored."

Their gazes shifted to the incoming ferry. Over the loud speaker, the captain called out, "Prepare to go ashore!" When it docked, several people stepped off.

Briony gently elbowed John. "Do you think those folks are here for a wedding, a funeral, or are they running from something?"

"We know they're not here for Colleen's funeral since her body hasn't been found yet."

"Nor has Mira's. But Chief Pemberton told me he'd contact me if and when her body washes up. I want to pay for her to be buried next to my father."

"That's a generous gesture, Briony. You really do have a heart of gold." John's dark eyes lit up. "Hey, you remembered what I told you about visitors to Cape Marble."

Her mouth curved into a smile. "I remember every conversation we've had."

He leaned into her. His lips grazed her neck before he whispered into her ear, "As have I. And I've no doubt there'll be many more fascinating conversations yet to come. If you'll let me, I plan to visit you in Kansas. All you need to do is send me an invitation."

Briony's hand fluttered at her chest. There'd been too many years spent building herself a bulwark against the black spaces of her past. Now John was in her life. He was a healing balm for the gaping wounds in her heart.

The day they'd met, she'd had the most peculiar sensation, as if something inside her had recognized him. She hadn't wanted to admit it until now. Getting close to a man had been another fear, but it was one that no longer existed. In her heart, John possessed all that she'd dreamed of. From the passion that clouded his face, she suspected she might be the girl he'd been waiting for, too.

She never imagined love could happen so fast. But when she held this man's gaze, she almost let herself believe in a happily ever after.

"All aboard that's coming aboard!" shouted the ferry captain.

"That's me," she said.

When John placed the suitcase in her hand, their hands touched, and an electric current pulsed between them. He threaded his fingers underneath her hair to cradle her head, and then he gave her a long lingering kiss.

Their mouths parted, and she felt herself drowning in the depths of his eyes. "Goodbye, John."

He shook his head. "It's not goodbye for us, Briony. You're heading out alone today, but our journey together is only beginning."

Cries in the Mist

She smiled knowingly, and then walked across the plank bridge and stepped upon the ferry. Despite the cool breeze teasing her hair, a flame blazed through her. She stood at the rail and waved as the boat pulled away from the dock. John waved back.

"We'll see each other soon!" he called.

She nodded, unable to stop joyous tears from pricking her eyes.

With each chug, the ferry moved farther away from Cape Marble. And still, John remained firmly planted on the dock. Feeling as if she'd ascended into a dream, she pulled her father's binoculars from the bag on her shoulder and peered through the lens. Her gaze landed on John's figure, and her heart jumped when he blew her a kiss.

When at last he was but a tiny speck in her vision, she slowly shifted the binoculars away from the dock and toward the lighthouse. It was a clear and beautiful autumn day. She moved them slowly up and down the structure. There was no mist shrouding the tower like the first time she'd laid eyes upon it. In fact, the lighthouse itself no longer appeared to be weathered and chipped. Although Briony knew it couldn't be possible, it seemed to shine with renewal.

She squinted. A woman in a long blue dress stood at the rail on the observation deck. Tiny crystals of shimmering light moved together around her like a giant rolling wave before morphing into dozens of individual spirit babies. All of their eyes were closed and all had tiny smiles etched upon their faces. The crying seemed to have ended once and for all.

Briony's father appeared behind Mira. He waved, and Briony exhaled a gentle rush of air and waved back. Her eyes fluttered shut. When they opened again, the observation deck was empty.

She lowered the binoculars and took a seat on one of the wooden benches. No longer as afraid of the ocean as before, she stared over the rail at the waves lapping against the boat and smiled, remembering how Ben had always loved the water.

From inside her shoulder bag, the edge of the picture frame she'd taken from the light keeper's cottage poked her rib. She didn't think her father would mind. It was the one of him with her and Ben. Once she got home, it would find its place on her bedside table. And hopefully, there'd be a photo of her and John sitting beside it in the not so distant future.

ABOUT THE AUTHOR

Staccy Coverstone is a multi-published author of Gothics, mysteries, ghost stories, romantic suspense, and western romance. She lives in Maryland with her husband, their dogs and cats, and a paint horse named Bill. They have two grown daughters and a baby granddaughter. When she's not writing, Stacey enjoys reading, photography, target shooting, traveling, and making scrapbooks of her adventures.

If you'd like to be informed when she has a new book release, please feel free to join her Announce Only Newsletter.

Please visit her Website at:
http://www.staceycoverstone.com.

Made in the USA
Columbia, SC
06 November 2025